Mare Ultima

Mare Ultima

Alex Irvine

Mare Ultima

Cover Art

Published in February 2012 by PS Publishing Ltd. by arrangement with the author.

First Edition

ISBN

978-1-848632-94-3

978-1-848632-95-0 (signed)

Design by Jupper Peep

www.jupperpeep.com

Printed in England by MPG Books Group

PS Publishing Ltd / Grosvenor House / 1 New Road / Hornsea / HU18 1PG / England

editor@pspublishing.co.uk / www.pspublishing.co.uk

Mare Ultima

I: The Tomb

They brought the singer to the obsidian gate and waited. A sandstorm began to boil in the valley that split the mountains to their west. Across the miles of desert, they watched it rear and approach. Still the singer did not sing. She was blind, and had the way of blind singers. They were as much at the mercy of the song as anyone else.

All of them were going to die in the sandstorm. At least the guard captain, Paulus, hoped so. If the sandstorm did not kill them, whatever was in the tomb would. Of the two deaths, he much preferred the storm. Two fingers of his right hand touched his throat and he hummed the creed of his god, learned from the Book at the feet of a mother he had not seen since his eighth year. The reflex was all that mattered. The first moon, still low over the mountains, vanished in the storm a moment after the mountains themselves.

The singer began to sing. Paulus hated her for it, but with the song begun, even killing her would not stop it. In one of the libraries hung the severed head of a singer, in a cage made of her bones. No one living could remember who she was, or understand the language of the song. The scholars of the court believed that whoever deciphered the song would know immortality.

They were at the mouth of a valley that snaked down from the mountains and spilled into a flat plain that once had been a marsh, a resting place for migrating birds. The tomb's architect, according to the scholars, had believed that the soul's migration was eased by placing the tomb in such a place. In the centuries since the death of the king, his world had also died. The river that fed the marshes shifted course to the south; the desert swept in. Paulus scanned the sky and saw no birds.

At first he found the song pleasing. The melody was unfamiliar to him, in a mode that jarred against the songs he remembered from his boyhood. Then all the gates in his mind boomed shut again. He was not a boy taken into the king's service who remembered the songs his mother might have sung. He was the guard captain Paulus and he was here in the desert to have the singer sing her song, and then to die.

Why, they had not been told. The tomb was to be opened. Paulus was a soldier. He would open the tomb. In doing so, he would die, but Paulus did not fear death. He had faced it in forms seen by few other men, had survived its proximity often enough that it had grown familiar. Fatalism was an old friend. The song made his teeth hurt; no, not the song, but some effect of the song. In this place, it was awakening something that had slumbered since The Fells was a scattering of huts on the riverbank. This king had died so long ago that his name was lost. At his death the desert had been green. The world changed, aged with the rest of them. In the desert, you breathed the air of a world where everything had happened already, and it made you feel that you could never have existed.

The obsidian gate shifted with a groan and the wind rose. Sand cascaded down the walls, revealing worked stone, as the singer's song began the work of undoing a burial that had taken the desert centuries to complete. The dozen soldiers with Paulus shifted on their feet, casting glances back and forth between the gate and the approaching storm. They rested hands on sword hilts, gauged the distance to their horses; Paulus could see each of them running through a delicate personal calculation, with the storm on one side and a deserter's crucifixion on the other.

At the mouth of the tomb, at the end of his life, Paulus had only gossip to steer by. Someone important, a merchant named Jan who had the king's ear, wanted to free the spirit that inhabited the tomb. The king had agreed. Paulus wondered what favor he owed that made him willing to cast away the lives of a dozen men. Perhaps they would not die. Still, they had ridden nine days across the desert, to a tomb so old and feared that it existed on maps only through inference; the desert road bent sharply away from it, cutting upward to run along the spine of a line of hills to the north before coming back down into the valley and following the ancient riverbed up to the Salt Pass, from which a traveler could see the ocean on a clear day. Paulus wondered what in the tomb had convinced the road builders believe that three days' extra ride was worth it.

The singer wept, whether in ecstasy or sorrow Paulus could not tell. Swirls of sand reared in the figures of snakes all around them, striking away in the rising wind. The obsidian gate was open an inch. The wind scoured sand away from the front of the tomb, revealing a path of flat stones. Another inch of darkness opened up. The singer's vibrato shook slivers from the gate that swept away over their heads like slashes of ink inscribed on the sky. Slowly the gate shivered open, grinding across the stones as the singer began to scream. The soldiers broke and ran; Paulus let them go, to die in whatever way they found best. A sound came from the tomb, answering the singer, and the harmony of voices living and dead burst Paulus' eardrums. Deaf, he felt the wind beat his face. Darkness fell as the storm swallowed the sky. The air grew thick as saliva. The sand undulated like a tongue. From the open gate of the tomb, Paulus smelled the exhalation of an undead spirit. He drew his sword, and then the sandstorm overtook them.

When it had passed, Paulus fumbled for the canteen at his belt. He rinsed his eyes, swished water around in his mouth and spat thick black gunk . . . onto a floor of even stones. He was in the tomb, without memory of having entered. Water dripped from his beard and he felt the scrape and grind of sand all over his body. He was still deaf. His eardrums throbbed. Where was the rest of the guard? He turned in a slow circle, orienting himself, and stopped when he was facing the open doorway. A featureless sandscape, brushed smooth by the storm and suffused with violet moonlight, stretched to an invisible horizon. The skin on the back of Paulus' neck crawled. He turned back to face into the tomb, growing curious. He enough oil for a torch. Its light seemed a protective circle to him as he ventured into the tomb to see what might have been left behind when the spirit emerged into the world. What it might do was no concern of his. He had been sent to free it; it was free. The merchant in The Fells had what he had paid for.

Torch held off to his left, sword in his right hand, Paulus walked down the narrow entry hall. He went down a stairway and at the bottom found the open sepulcher. The ancient king's bones lay as they had been left. His hair wisped over a mail coat that caught the torchlight.

Am I to be a graverobber? Paulus thought. The spirit was fled. Why not?

He took a cutting of the king's hair, binding it with a bit of leather from the laces of his jerkin. Arrayed about the king's body were ceremonial articles: a sword pitted and brittle with age, jars which had once held spices and perfumes, the skeletons of a dog and a child. Paulus went through it all, keeping what he knew he could sell and ignoring anything that looked as if it might be infected with magic. He worked methodically, feeling distanced from himself by his deafness. After an hour's search through the main room of the tomb and an antechamber knee-deep in sand from the storm, he had a double handful of gold coins. Everything else he saw—a sandstone figurine with obsidian eyes, a jeweled torc obscured by the king's beard, a filigreed scroll case laid diagonally into a wall alcove just inside the door—made him leery of enchantment. The gold would do.

Leaving the tomb, he stumbled over the body of the singer, buried in a drift of sand just inside the shattered gate. There was no sign of the rest of his men. It disturbed Paulus that he had no memory of entering the tomb as the storm broke over them, but memory was a blade with no handle. When it failed, best to live with the failure and live to accumulate new memories. He took another drink, scanned the desert for sign of the horses, and gave up. Either he would walk back, or he could cross the mountains and sail around the Cape of Thirst from the city of Averon. The boat would be quicker and the coastal waters less treacherous than the desert sands. Paulus turned west.

II: THE FELLS

In three days, he was coming down the other side of the pass. Two days after that, he was sleeping in the shadow of wine casks on the deck of a ship called *Furioso*. On the twelfth day after walking out of the tomb, Paulus stepped off the gangplank into the dockside chaos of The Fells, and wound his way through the city toward the Ridge of the Keep. He wondered how the merchant Jan would know that the spirit was freed, and also how Mikal, the Marshal of the King's Guard, would react to the loss of his men.

To be the sole survivor of a battle, or of an expedition, was to be assumed a liar. Paulus knew this. He could do nothing about it except tell what portion of the truth would serve him. Any soldier learned that truths told to superiors were necessarily partial.

Mikal received his report without surprise, in fact without much reaction at all. "Understood," he said at the end of Paulus' tale. "His Majesty anticipated the possibility of such losses. You have done well to return." Mikal wrote in the log of the guard. Paulus waited. When he was done writing, Mikal said, "You will return to regular duties once you have repeated your story for Jan Destrier."

So Paulus walked back through The Fells, from the Ridge of the Keep down into the market known as the Jingle and then upriver past the quay where he had disembarked from *Furioso*, to tell his story to a man named for a horse. In the Jingle he remembered where as a boy he performed acrobatics for pennies, and where his brother Piero had saved his life by changing him into a dog and then saved it again by trading one of his eyes for a spell. Paulus had not seen his brother in years. So much in one life, he thought. I was a boy, feeding chickens and playing at being a pirate. Then I was in The Fells, rejected from the King's service. Then I did serve the King, and still do. I have fought in his wars, and killed the men he wanted killed, and now I have released the spirit of a dead king into the world to satisfy an arrangement whose details I will never know.

But whom have I ever stood for the way Piero stood for me?

Jan Destrier's shopfront faced the river across a cobblestoned expanse that was part street and part quay. There was no sign, but Paulus had been told to look for a stuffed heron in the doorway. He could not remember who had told him. Mikal? Unease roiled his stomach, but his step was sure and steady as he crossed the threshold into Jan Destrier's shop. The merchant was behind a counter through whose glass top Paulus could see bottles of cut crystal in every shape, holding liquids and pooled gases that caught the light of a lantern hung over Jan Destrier's head. He was a large man, taller than Paulus and fat in the way men allowed themselves to get fat when their lives permitted it. At first Paulus assumed the bottles held perfume; then he saw the alchemical array on a second table behind the merchant and he understood. Jan Destrier sold magic.

At once Paulus wanted to run, but he was not the kind of man who ran, perhaps because he did not value his life highly enough to abase himself for its sake. He hated magic, hated its unpredictability and the supercilious unction of the men who brokered its sale, hated even more the wizards of the Agate Tower who bound the lives of unknowing men to their own and from the binding drew their power. Once, drunk, Paulus and a groom in the castle stables named Andrew had found themselves arguing over the single best thing a king could do upon ascending the throne. Andrew, hardheaded and practical, wanted a decisive war with the agitating brigands in the mountains to the north; Paulus wanted every wizard and spell broker in The Fells put to the sword. The conversation had started off stupid and gotten worse as the bottle got lighter.

Now here he was in the shop of a broker, sent by a superior on business that concerned the king. Paulus could spit the broker on his sword and watch him die in the facets of his crystal bottles, but he himself would die shortly after. It was not his kingdom and never would be. He was obligated to carry out the orders he had been given.

"Jan Destrier," he said. "Mikal the king's marshal sent me to you."

"You must have something terribly important to tell me, then," Destrier said. "Tell it."

"I led a detachment of the guard out into the desert, where the Salt Pass Road bends away from the dry riverbed," Paulus said. "We had a singer with us. She opened a tomb, and the spirit of the king buried there was freed." He felt like he should add something about the deaths of the singer and his men, but Jan Destrier would not care. "As you requested," he finished.

"There has been a misunderstanding," Destrier said. "I did not wish the spirit to escape."

Paulus inclined his head. "Beg pardon, that was the order I received."

"As may be." Destrier beckoned Paulus around the counter. "Come here." Paulus did, and the merchant stopped him when he had cleared the counter. "What I wanted was for the spirit to come here. That was what the singer was for. Well, partly."

"Then permit me to convey my regrets at the failure of the King's Guard," Paulus said. "The spirit came out of the tomb, but I did not see it after that. There was a storm."

"I'm sure there was," Destrier said. "There almost always is. Never fear, the spirit arrived just as I had hoped." He held up a brass instrument, all curls and notched edges. Paulus had never seen its like before. "You were kind enough to bring it along with you. Or, perhaps I should say that it was kind enough to bring you along with it."

No, Paulus thought. If the spirit was there, then it saw me robbing the tomb. He closed his fingers around the cutting of the king's hair, thinking that if he could destroy the fetish—crisp it in one of the candle flames that burned along the edges of the merchant's table—that perhaps the spirit would no longer be able to find him. Already he was too late. The spirit, enlivened by some magnetism of the merchant's, drained the strength from his hands. Paulus felt the whisper of its soul in his brain, like the echo of wind in the black silence of a tomb. His legs were the next to go. His arms jerked out looking for something to hold onto, but nothing was there, and when the numbness crept past his knees, Paulus crumpled to the floor. He felt the paralysis like a drug, spinning his mind away from his body until at last he lost touch even with his senses and fell into a dream that was like dying.

"I thought it would ride the singer," Jan Destrier said. "How odd that it chose you instead."

He did not know how long the stupor lasted. When he regained his senses, everything about him was as it had been before: the table littered with alchemical vessels and curling parchment, the border of pinprick candle flames, the batwing eyebrows of the merchant shadowing his eyes. The merchant looked up as Paulus stirred. "You have performed admirably," he said. "It's not every man who would have survived the initial possession, and even fewer live to tell of the extraction."

There would be nothing to tell, Paulus thought. He had no memory of it.

"Where has the spirit gone, then?" he asked. It would come for him, of that he was sure. It had ridden him back to The Fells and now that it was free it would exact some revenge for his spoliation of its tomb. Perhaps it would ride him back, if by coming it had fulfilled whatever geas the merchant had laid on it. Then it would abandon him in the sands to die, the way he had thought he would die when the first notes of the singer's song had begun to resonate in the stones of the tomb.

"I have it here." Destrier produced a cucurbit stoppered with wax, and filled with a swirling fluid. "The stopper is made from the catalyst. When I apply heat, it will melt into the impure spirit, and the reaction will precipitate the spirit into another glass. This essence is my stock in trade. You are familiar with the magic market?"

"I know of it," Paulus said. "I have never made use of it." This was a lie, but Paulus had no compunction about lying to merchants, who were in his experience congenital liars. Twice in his life, his brother had spent magic on him.

"Well, do keep me in mind if you ever find yourself in need," the merchant said.

Paulus' curiosity got the better of him. He framed his question carefully, already outlining a strategy for evading and defeating the spirit. But first he had to know as much as possible about its nature. "Is there magic in the spirit because it died having not used its own? How do you know it has any?"

"Magic is more complicated than the nursery rhymes and old wives' tales would have it," the merchant said. "Yes, every human is born with a spark, and may use it. But other forms of enchantment and power inhere in the world. In stones, in articles touched by great men or tainted by proximity to unexpected death. These can be refined, their magic distilled and used. This is what I do. In the case of spirits, and whether their magic results from unused mortal power or something else," he went on, "it is not what the mathematicians would call a zero-sum endeavor. By trapping the spirit, I trap the potential for its magic that it has brought back from the other world. Distilled and processed, this magic can be sold just as any other. Although the nature of the spirit makes such magics unsuitable for certain uses."

The echoes of the possession still sounded in the hollows of Paulus' mind. He heard the merchant without active understanding. "We are finished here?" he asked.

"Quite," the merchant said. "Do convey my commendation of your performance to your superior officers."

"A commendation would carry more weight coming from yourself," Paulus said.

The merchant scribbled on a parchment, folded it, and sealed it. "Then let us hope the weight of it does not overburden you," he said. Paulus left him setting small fires under the alembic that would purify the spirit's essence into a salable bit of magic.

He delivered the merchant's commendation to Mikal because not to do so would have been stupid. Then he set about shaping a plan to get that distilled element of magic back from the merchant before he sold it, and in its use an unsuspecting client became a tool for the spirit's vengeance on Paulus. He did not have enough money to buy the magic and knew that he could not trade his own; the essence of the undead spirit was doubtless more powerful. He could take it by force, but he would have to kill the merchant, and then leave The Fells—and the King's service—forever. The cowardice of this path repelled him. He owed the King his life. Twice over. He did not love the King, but Paulus understood obligation.

It was obligation that brought him to the seneschal's chamber after word of the merchant's commendation circulated through the court. Mario Tremano had once been the king's tutor. Now much of the court's business was quietly transacted by means of his approval. He was a careful man, an educated man, and a cruel man. Paulus feared him the way he feared all men who loved subtlety. It was tradition in The Fells for scholars to wield influence, but it was also tradition for them to overreach; as Piero often joked, the scholar's stooped posture cried out for straightening on the gallows. Paulus went to Mario Tremano's chamber wondering if Jan Destrier's commendation had made him useful, or doomed him. The only way to find out was to go.

Nearing seventy years of age, Mario cultivated the appearance of a scholar despite his wealth and the raw unspoken fact of his power. He wore a scholar's simple gown and black cap, and did not braid his beard or hair. "Paulus," he said as his footman escorted Paulus into his study. "You have attracted attention from powerful friends of the King."

"I have always tried to serve the King," Paulus said.

"And serve the King you have," Mario said with a smirk. Paulus noted the insult and folded into his understanding of his situation. It was hardly the first time he had heard cutting remarks about the part of his life he'd spent as a dog. The more venomous ladies of the court still occasionally yipped when they passed him in the castle's corridors. Eleven years had done little to dull the appeal of the joke. The seneschal paused, as if waiting for Paulus to react to the slight. "Now, in our monarch's autumn years, you have a glorious chance to perform a most unusual service," he went on.

"However I may," Paulus said. He had heard that the king was unwell, but Mario's open acknowledgment suggested that the royal health was on unsteadier footing than Paulus had known. He was ten years older than Paulus, and should still have been in the graying end of his prime.

"Your willingness speaks well of you, Captain." Mario spread a map on a table below a window that faced out over The Fells and weighted its edges with candlesticks. Paulus saw the broad estuary of the Black River, with The Fells on its western side. The great Cape of Thirst swept away to the southwest, ending in a curl sheltering Averon. To the north and west, Paulus saw names of places where he had fought in the king's wars: Kiriano, Ie Fure, the Valley of Caves. This was the first time he had ever seen such a map. It made the world seem at once larger, because so much of it Paulus had never seen, and smaller, because it could be encompassed on a sheet of vellum.

The seneschal tapped a location far to the north. *Mare Ultima*, Paulus read. "How long do you think it would take you to get there?"

Paulus looked at the distance between The Fells and Averon, which was twelve days on horse. Then he gauged the distance from The Fells to Mario's fingertip, taking into account the two ranges of mountains. "Six weeks," he guessed. "Or as much as eight if the weather is bad."

"The weather will be bad," Mario said. "Of that you can be sure. Winter falls in September in that country."

It was late in June. Paulus waited for the seneschal to continue his geography lesson, but a sharp question from the chamber door interrupted them. "What have you told him?"

Paulus was kneeling as he turned, the rich tones of the queen's voice acting on his muscles before his brain registered what had been said. He dared not look at her, for fear that he would fall in love as his brother had. This fear had accompanied him for the past eleven years, since he had reawakened into humanity. She had done it, bought the magic to restore his human form, as a reward to his brother for his long service as the king's fool. His brother was blind now, and loved the queen for her voice and her scent and the sound of her gown sweeping along the stone floors. Paulus carried a mosaic of her in his head: the fall of her hair, caught in a thin shaft of sunlight; a line at the corner of her mouth, which had taught Paulus much about the passage of years; a time when an ermine stole slipped from her shoulder and Paulus caught his breath at the sight of her pulse in the hollow of her throat. He believed that if he ever looked her full in the face, and held her gaze for a heartbeat, that love would consume him.

"Your Majesty," Mario said. "He has as yet only heard a bit about the seasons in the north."

"Rise, Captain," the queen said. Paulus did, keeping his eyes low. To the seneschal, the queen said, "Well. Perhaps you should tell him what we are about to ask him to do."

"Of course, Your Majesty. Captain, what stories have you heard about dragons?"

Paulus looked up at the seneschal. "Of dragons? The same stories as any child, Excellency. I think."

Mario retrieved a book from a shelf behind his desk. He set it on the map and opened it. "A natural history," he said. "Written by the only man I know who has ever seen a dragon. A source we can trust. Can you write?"

Paulus nodded.

"Then you must copy this," Mario said, "while we instruct you in the details of your task."

Paulus took up a quill and began to write. *Dragons are solitary beasts, powerful as whales and cunning as an ape. They mate in flight only, and the females are never seen except at these moments. Where they nest and brood, no man knows . . .* At some point during the lesson that followed, the queen touched Paulus on the shoulder. It felt like a blessing, an expression of faith. His unattainable lady who had given him back the shape of a man was now setting him a quest, and though he would probably die, he would undertake the quest feeling that she had offered him a destiny.

His task was this: in the broken hills between the northernmost range of mountains and the icy Mare Ultima, there lived a dragon. *Extremes of heat and cold are the dragon's love. In caves of ice and on the shoulders of volcanoes, there may they be found in numbers.* Once, before ascending the throne, the king had hunted it, and survived the failure of the hunt. It was the queen's wish that before he died, her husband should know that he had outlived the dragon. *A dragon might live hundreds of years. No man can be certain, because no man lives as long as a dragon.* It was to be her death-gift to him, in thanks for the years they had spent as man and wife. "He has lived a life as full as mortal might wish," she said. "Yet this memory hounds him, and I would not have it hound him when he is in his grave."

"Your Majesty, it will not," Paulus said. Whether he meant that he believed he would kill the dragon, or meant only that worldly desires did not accompany spirits, he could not have said. *Many tales and falsehoods exist regarding magical properties of the dragon's blood. These include . . .*

"How are we to know it is done?" the seneschal said.

"What token would His Majesty wish, as proof of the deed?" Paulus asked the queen. He kept his eyes on the page, and the nib of the quill wet. . . . *language of birds, which some believe to derive their origin from a lost race of smaller dragons quite gone from the world.*

"On the king's thigh is a scar from the dragon's teeth," she said, "and under his hair a scar from its tail. I would have its long teeth and the tip of its tail. The rest you may keep. I care not for whatever treasure it might hoard."

In fact, according to the seneschal's book, dragons did not hoard treasure. *They care not for gold or jewels, but such may be found in their dens if left by those who try to kill a dragon and fail. It is said that such treasure grows cursed from being in the dragon's presence, but place no faith in this superstition.* Paulus copied this information down without relaying it to the queen. "Captain," Mario said. "Jan Destrier spoke well enough of you that you perhaps should visit him before you embark. He certainly would have something to assist you."

"Many thanks, Excellency," Paulus said. "Would it be possible to put something in writing, that there is no confusion on the merchant's part?"

"I hope you do not express doubt as to my word," the seneschal said.

Although the dragon is said to speak, it does not. Some are said to mimic sounds made in their presence, as do parrots and other talking birds, but I do not know if this is true. Paulus was almost done copying the pages. His hand hurt. He could not remember ever having written three pages at once. "Beg pardon, no, Excellency," he said. "I doubt only the merchant's memory and attachment to his wares, and I have no gold to buy what he refuses to give."

This was a carefully shaded truth. Gold Paulus had; whether it was enough to buy any useful magic, he did not know.

"Well said, Captain," the queen commented.

The seneschal was silent. Out of the corner of his eye, Paulus could see that he was absolutely still. Paulus' soldier instinct began to prickle on the back of his neck and he hesitated in his copying as his hand reflexively began to reach for his sword. There was bad blood in the room. *It is said that a dragon recognizes the man who will kill it, and this is the only man it will flee. Contrary to this saying, I have never observed a fleeing dragon, nor expect to.* Paulus would never be able to prove it, but in that instant he knew that when the king passed from this world, Mario Tremano would attempt to send his widow quickly after. He resolved without a second thought to kill the seneschal when he returned from his errand to the Mare Ultima. *The dragon's scale is fearsome strong, and will deflect nearly any blade or bolt, but its weaknesses are: inside the joints of the legs, near the anus, the eyes, under the hinges of the jaw.*

"Yes. Apparently being around the court has taught you some tricks, Captain. You must leave immediately," Mario said when Paulus finished copying. He handed Paulus a folded and sealed letter. It could have been a death warrant for all Paulus knew. "Our king must know that this is done, and his time is short."

Paulus rose to leave, rolling the copied pages into a tight scroll that he slid under his belt. Twice now, the seneschal had slighted him. "You may choose any horse," the queen said. "And the armory is yours."

"Your Majesty's generosity humbles me," Paulus said.

"Apparently so much that you act the peasant in my presence," she said, a bit archly. "Will you not look me in the face, Captain Paulus of the King's Guard?"

I would, Paulus thought. How I would. "Your Majesty," he said, "I fear that if I did, I would be unable to go from you, and would prove myself unworthy of your faith in me."

"He certainly is loyal," said Mario the seneschal. Paulus took his leave, right hand throbbing, slighted a third time in front of his queen. One day it would come to blades between him and the seneschal.

That was a battle that could not yet be fought. First, he must survive a long trip to the north and a battle with a dragon. It was said that only a king or a hero could kill a dragon. Paulus was not a king and he did not know if he was a hero. He had fought eleven years of wars, had killed men of every color in every territorial hinterland and provincial capital claimed by The Fells, had survived wounds that he had seen kill other men. Perhaps he had performed heroic deeds. If he survived the encounter with the dragon, the question would be put to rest.

He chose a steel-gray stallion from the stable, young but proven in the Ie Fure campaign the summer before. Andrew, emerging from the workshop where he repaired tack, said, "Paulus, you can't mean it. That one's Mikal's favorite."

"Andrew, friend, if the horse doesn't come back, I won't be coming, either. And if both of us do come back, I'll have the court at my feet. So I have nothing to worry about from Mikal either way."

"Court at your feet," Andrew repeated. "How's that?"

"The queen has sent me to kill a dragon." Paulus said.

"There's no such thing as dragons," Andrew said.

"The queen thinks there are, and she wants me to kill one of them." Paulus swung up onto the horse. "So I will. Now come with me to the armory."

Paulus had never fought with a lance, but he had thrown his share of spears. He took three, and a great sword with a blade twice as wide and a foot longer than the long sword he'd carried these past six years. He added a short butchering knife with a curve near the tip of its blade, which he imagined to be a better tool for digging out a dragon's teeth than his dagger. A sling, for hunting along the way, and a helmet, greaves, and gauntlets to go over the suit of mail that lay oiled and wrapped in canvas in one of Paulus' saddlebags. The book had said nothing about whether dragons could breathe fire. If they could, none of his preparations would make any difference.

"Two swords, spears, knives," Andrew said. "I'll wager a bottle you can kill it just with the sling."

"That's not a bet you make with a man you think is going to survive," Paulus said. Andrew didn't argue the point.

"If I'm not back by the first of November, I won't be back," Paulus said. He clasped hands with Andrew and rode out of the keep into the stinking bustle of The Fells. The sun was sinking toward the desert that began a half-day's ride west from the Black River's banks. Paulus thought of the tomb, and the spirit, and grew uncertain about the plan that was already forming in his head. Twenty minutes' ride through the city brought him to Jan Destrier's door. He tied the horse and went inside.

The spell broker was cleaning a tightly curled copper tube. "Ah, the bearer of spirits is returned," he said. "To purchase, no doubt."

Paulus held out the letter from Mario Tremano. After reading it, the broker said, "I see. I am to assist you."

"I am leaving on a quest given by the queen Herself," Paulus said.

"A quest. Oh my," Destrier said. "For what?"

"For something I will not be able to get without help from your stores."

"Specificity, O Captain of the Guard," Destrier said. "What is it you want? Luck? Do you wish not to feel cold, or fire? Thirst? Do you wish to be invisible, or to go nine days without sleep?"

"I wish the essence of the spirit I brought back to you," Paulus said.

Destrier laughed. "I might as well wish the queen's ankles locked around the back of my neck," he said. "We're both going to be disappointed."

It was not Paulus' life that mattered. Not his success or failure at killing the dragon. It was the murderous guile he had sensed in the presence of Mario Tremano and what that meant for the life of the queen after her husband was no longer there to be a useful asset to the seneschal. For her, Paulus would do anything. He stole nothing after killing Jan Destrier; he used the fetish of the dead king's hair to find the essence of the spirit, which was an inch of clear fluid in a brass bulb the size of a fig. He tied it around his neck with a piece of leather, threading the binding of the fetish into the knot that held the bulb.

There would be consequences. If Paulus brought back the teeth and tail of the dragon, he would survive them; if he did not, it would not matter. On the street, he made no effort to hurry. Most of those who had heard Jan Destrier die would be more interested in plundering his expensive wares than in reporting that the killer was dressed in the livery of the King's Guard. He rode for the North River Gate and out into the world beyond The Fells.

He did not know how much power was in the spirit's essence, or of what kind. He did not know whether any of its soul survived inside the brass bulb. But he had a token of the body it had once animated, and he had six weeks to find out.

III: The Quest

With ten days left in August, Paulus came down out of the mountains into the land that on Mario Tremano's map looked like a thin layer of fat between the mountains and the Mare Ultima. He had seen snow three times in the mountains already and heard an avalanche on a warm day after a heavy storm. He had been traveling fifty days. Twice he had cut his beard with the butchering knife. He had killed one man so far, for trying to steal his horse. Mikal's horse. He had hunted well, and so eaten well, and even traded some of his game for cheese and bread and the occasional piece of fruit at farmsteads and villages along the way.

He had also learned something of the nature of the spirit in the brass bulb that hung next to the fetish around his neck. If there was anything Paulus mistrusted more than magic, it was dreams, but nevertheless it was through dreams that he had begun to learn. He was sitting in front of a campfire built in the ribcage of a dragon, listening to the bones speak, telling him he knew nothing of dragons. Your book is full of lies, the voice said.

The Book is about faith and learning, Paulus replied, touching two fingers to his throat. The Journey and the Lesson. It was what his mother had taught him.

Idiot, the voice said. Your book about dragons is what I mean.

It may be, Paulus said.

It is.

He awoke from that first dream with the brass bulb unstoppered and held to his lips. "No," he said, and stoppered it again. "So you do know me."

He would have to be careful, he thought. Something of the spirit remained and he could not know whether it wished him good or ill. He would learn, and when the time came to face the dragon, he would hope he had learned enough.

The second dream took him after he rose in the night to piss into a creek in the foothills of the first mountain range that lay between him and the Mare Ultima. As he drifted back into sleep, he dreamed of walking out into that creek, trying to wash something from his skin that burned and sickened him. This is what you will feel, said the voice of the water over the rocks. This and much worse.

Paulus stopped and stood, dripping and naked, letting the feeling inhabit him, imagining what it would be like to withstand it and fight through it. How much worse? He asked . . . and woke screaming in a predawn fog, with the gray stallion a shadow rearing at the agony in his voice.

The night of the first snow, as he crested the first pass and descended into a valley bounded by canyons and glaciers that curved like ribs into sparkling tarns, he was reminded of the first dream. He cut a lean-to from tree branches and packed the snow over and around it, then huddled under his blanket with a small fire at the mouth of the lean-to. When he slept, the voice was the sound of tree branches cracking under the weight of snow. I have killed dragons.

What does that matter to me? You cannot kill this one for me, and even if you could, it would shame me to permit it.

Shame, the voice cackled. It looks very different when you are dead.

Someday I will know that, Paulus said. But not soon.

Sooner than you wish, unless you listen.

Then talk, so I can decide if what you say is worth listening to.

You cut hair from my body, and took gold from my tomb, the voice said.

All the more reason to be suspicious of you.

With a cackle, the voice said How much you think you know. Who guided you to the broker's? And when you came back to the broker's—

do you think you found me? No, mortal man. I brought you to me. I would kill a dragon again.

A cold, shameful fear made Paulus moan in his sleep. The queen—

No. Her mind is her own. I was a king, and would not meddle with others of my station. You, on the other handz . . .

Paulus woke up. In the pages he had copied from Mario Tremano's book, it was said that kings of old had killed dragons, and driven them to the wastes of the north and west. He rolled the brass bulb in his palms. The spirit had said that the book was full of lies. If the spirit told the truth, then kings of old had not killed dragons, which meant that the spirit was lying.

That is man's logic, he thought, remembering a story from the Book in which a man tried to reason with lightning. Yes, the lightning had said. There is no flaw in your thought, save that it is man's thought, and I am lightning.

Shaking out the blanket and refolding it over the horse's back, Paulus found himself in the same position. In a week, or perhaps ten days, he would find the dragon. Then he would discover which lies the spirit was telling.

With ten days left in August, he came down out of the mountains and began asking the questions. The people who hunted seals and caribou along the shores of Mare Ultima spoke a language he knew only from a few words picked up on campaigns, when mercenary companies had come down from this land of black rock and blue ice, bringing their spears and an indifference to suffering bred at the end of the world. He pieced together, over days, that there was a dragon, and that it slept in a cave formed after the eruption and collapse of a volcano. He worked his way across the country, eating white rabbits and salmon and the dried blubber of seals, building his strength, until he found the dragon's cave.

The mountain still smoked. Standing on a ridge that paralleled the shore, some miles distant, Paulus looked south. The mountains, already whitening. North: water the color of his stallion, broken by ice floes all the way to a misty horizon. East: coastal hills, green and gray speckled with snow. West: more mountains, their peaks shrouded in clouds. The people he had spoken to said that in the west, mountains burned.

This was as good a place as any to find a dragon, Paulus thought. As good a place as any to die.

The dragon's cave was a sleepy eye perhaps a half-mile up the ruined side of a mountain. The top of the mountain was scooped out, ringed with sharp spires; a waterfall drained what must have been an immense lake in the crater, carving a canyon down the mountainside and a new river through the hills to the Mare Ultima. Paulus could smell some kind of flower, and the ocean, and from somewhere far to the west the tang of smoke. He dismounted and began to prepare. First, the mail shirt, still slick with oil. Gauntlets, their knuckles squealing like the hinges of a door not hung true. Greaves buckled over his boots. The great sword across his back. Shield firm on his left forearm, spear in his right hand, long sword on his hip. The butchering knife sheathed behind his left hip.

Then he thought, No. This is man's thinking, and I am going to fight the lightning.

He stabbed the spear into the ground, and let the great sword fall from his back. Setting his shield down, Paulus took off the gauntlets. He snapped the leather thong around his neck and unwound the binding of the fetish. With the butchering knife, he cut a tangled lock of his own hair. There was more gray in it than he remembered from the last time he had looked in a mirror, but he was forty-five years old now. He twisted the two locks of hair together into a tangle of black and gray long enough that he could wind it around the base of the middle finger on his right hand, and then in a figure-eight around his thumb. He bound it in place, and unstoppered the bulb. As he tipped a few drops of the fluid onto the place where the figure-eight crossed itself, he heard the voices of ice and snow, rocks and water, bones of dragons. He put a gauntlet on his right hand over the charm and tipped a few more drops into its palm. The rest he sprinkled over the blade of the sword. Then he cast the bulb away clinking among the stones.

It would work or it would not. Picking up his shield and holding his sword before him, Paulus picked his way at an angle up the slope toward the dragon's cave. A voice in his head said, *Now you know why I did not ride the singer.*

◆ ◆ ◆

Afterward, he was screaming, and when she came to him, he thought he was being guided out of his life. She spoke, and soothed him, and left him there in his own blood, writhing as the dragon's poison ate its way under his skin. The spirit was gone. In the echoes of its departure Paulus felt the slash of the dragon's claws, shredding his mail shirt and the muscle underneath. When his body spasmed with each fresh wave of poisoned agony, the grating of the mail links on the stone floor of the cave was the sound of the dragon's scales as it uncoiled and raised its head to meet him. The white of his femur and his ribs was the white of its bared fangs crushing his shield and snapping the bones in his wrist. And when he arched his back in seizure, as the poison worked deeper into his body, the impact of his head on the ground was the blinding slap of its tail and then the shock of his blade, driven home and snapped off in the hollow underneath its front leg. The dragon was dead and Paulus soon would be. He thrashed his right arm, flinging the bloody gauntlet away, and caught the fetish in his teeth. His face was slick with the dragon's blood and his own tears. Gnawing the fetish loose, he spat it out. Free, he thought. Free to die my own death. O my queen . . .

And she was back, with a sledge freshly cut and smelling of sap. Paulus recognized the language she spoke, but couldn't pick out the words. When she dragged him over the stones at the mouth of the cave, pain blew him out like a candle.

The next thing he could remember was the sound of wind, and the weight of a fur blanket, and the rank sweat of his body. He was inside, in a warm place. A creeping icy draft chilled his face. Paulus opened his eyes. The woman was stirring something in a pot over a fire. He tried to sit up and his wounds reawakened. The sound that came out of him was the sound wounded enemies made when the camp women went around the battlefield to kill them. The woman laid her bone spoon across the lip of the pot and came over to squat next to him. "Shhhhh," she said. Black, black hair, Paulus thought. And black, black eyes. Then he was gone again.

It was quiet and dark when next he awoke. He heard the woman breathing nearby. He flexed his fingers, wondering that he could still feel all ten. Under the blanket, he began to explore his body. His left wrist was bound and splinted, and radiated the familiar pain of a healing broken bone. Heavy scabs covered the right side of his body from just below his shoulder all the way down to the knee. He wiggled his toes. Something was sticking out of the scabs, and after puzzling over it Paulus realized that the woman—or someone—had stitched the worst of his wounds, with what he could not tell. He was going to live. He knew the smell of infection and his nose could not find it. He had clean wounds. Bad wounds, but clean. They would heal. He would walk, and he would live. He saw details in the near-perfect darkness of the room: the last embers in the fire pit, the swell of the woman under her blankets. His fingers roamed over his body, feeling the pebbled scars where the dragon's poison had burned him and the strangely smooth expanses that were without wounds. He flexed the muscles of his arms, and they hurt, but they worked. When he moved his legs, the deep tears in his right thigh cried out. Not healed yet, then. Putting that together with the way his wrist felt, Paulus guessed that it had been two weeks since the woman had found him in the mouth of the dragon's cave.

The teeth, he thought. And the tail.

He must not fail the queen.

"The dragon," he said to the woman the next morning. She shushed him. "I have to—"

Again she shushed him. Paulus sank back into the pile of furs and skins. He still had no strength. He watched her move around, taking in the details of her home. It was made of stone and wood, the spaces between the stones stuffed with moss and earth. One wall was a single slab of stone; a hillside, with three manmade walls completing the enclosure. Timbers slanted from the opposite wall to rest against the natural wall, covered with densely woven branches. Paulus couldn't believe it could contain warmth, but it did. He threw his covers off, suddenly sweating in the fur cocoon. The woman did not react to Paulus' nakedness. She opened a door he hadn't noticed and the interior of the house lit up with sunlight reflected from deep drifts of snow. The snow must be waist-deep, Paulus thought. Perhaps the dragon's cave was buried. Perhaps no one here wanted trophies from its carcass. Exhausted again, he did not resist when the woman settled covers back over him and went about her business. "Why did you save me?" Paulus asked her.

She shushed him, and again he fell asleep.

Gradually over the winter he learned more of her language, and she bits and pieces of his. From this he learned that she had hauled him to her home, put him on the pile of furs, and tended his wounds with skill that few surgeons in The Fells possessed. Or she was fortunate, and Paulus was strong. Perhaps he would have lived in any case, given shelter and food. He would never know.

His horse was outside, kept in an overhung spot along the bluffs that also made up the fourth wall of the house. As soon as he was strong enough, he went out to see it and found that someone in this icy wilderness knew something about horses; it was brushed, its hooves were trimmed. If these people had mastered ironworking, Paulus thought, the horse would have new shoes. The hospitality was humbling. He thanked her and asked her to thank whoever had taken care of the horse. About the dragon, she appeared confused when he finally made her understand that he had traveled for two months just to get pieces of it to take home. "For my queen," he said. Though she understood the words, the concept made no sense to her. Arguing with lightning, Paulus thought. Her name meant Joy in her language. She lived alone. Her mother and father were dead, and this was their house. In the good weather months, she fished and wove and tanned hides; in the winter, she kept to herself and wove cloth to sell the next summer. There was a village twenty minutes' walk away. A man there wanted to marry her, but she would not have him. He was the one who had cared for the stallion.

Paulus thanked her again. She shrugged. What else would she have done?

Growing stronger, he went out into the snow dressed in clothes Joy made. He met a few of the villagers, who lost interest in him as soon as they confirmed that he had not made Joy his wife. The dragon, it seemed, had made little difference in their lives. It ate caribou and sea lions. There were plenty of both to go around. In The Fells, should he survive to return there, Paulus would be celebrated; here, he was a curiosity.

On one of the first spring days, smells of the earth heavy in his nose, Paulus went out from Joy's house with the butchering knife tucked in his belt. He found his way to the dragon's cave and went inside. It lay more or less as he had left it. His broken sword blade, its edges now rusted, protruded from behind its left front leg. Marveling, Paulus paced off the length of its body. Fifty feet. It was mostly still frozen. He laid out the canvas sheet he'd used to protect his armor and set to work hacking into the carcass with the butchering knife. Four fangs for the queen, and the tip of the tail. Then he gouged out most of the rest of its teeth, leaving those that broke as he worked them free of the jawbone. In the pages he had copied from Mario Tremano's book were recipes for alchemical uses of the dragon's eyes, as well as a notation that its heart was said to confer the strength of giants. The eyes came out easily enough; the heart was another matter. Paulus went to work prying loose the scales on its breast until he could crack through its ribs. The heart, larger than his head, was pierced six inches deep by the blade of his sword. Sweating in the cold, he cut it out and put it with the eyes. Then he added several dozen of its scales, each the size of his spread hand.

When he was done, he walked back to Joy, who was outside bartering a roll of cloth for the haunch of a moose killed by a villager who would have gladly given her the haunch, and anything else, if she would accept him. That night, Joy and Paulus ate moose near the fire. When they were done, she got up to put the bowls in water. He handed her his dagger, slick with grease, and she looked at it for a moment before slashing it across his right forearm.

Paulus sprang away from her, hand instinctively dropping toward a sword hilt that wasn't there. "Joy!" he shouted, squaring off against her, glancing around for something he could use as a weapon. He had no doubt that he could overpower her, even weak as he still was, but no man ever went unarmed against an opponent with a knife if there was even a stick nearby that could improve the odds.

She pointed at his forearm. Unable to help himself, he looked. The skin was unmarked. Paulus looked back at her. She made no move to approach him; after a moment, she turned and dropped the knife into the pot of water with the bowls.

It is said of the dragon's blood that washing in it renders human flesh invulnerable to blade or arrow, the seneschal's book had said. Paulus had read over those lines the way he had the rest of the more fanciful passages, skeptically and with no effort to keep them in mind. But it was true. He had felt the blade hit his arm. It should have opened him up to the bone.

"Dragon," Joy said, and began to wash the dishes.

She knew, Paulus thought. She was showing him. Not just the transformation of his skin wetted with the dragon's lifeblood; she was showing him that he had survived.

"How," he began, and stopped when he realized he had too many questions to ask, and no words to ask them, and that she had no words to answer. He watched her dry his dagger and set it aside on the table. Before she could pick up another dish, he caught her wrist and drew her toward him. Her expression changed and he thought she would pull away, but she let him draw her down into the furs. She kept her eyes locked on his. Paulus—who had once been a dog, and who had spoken to the dead, and who had winterlong danced on the line between life and death—knew that when she looked into his eyes, she was seeing a dead man she had once loved.

For him, too, she was someone else. The spill of her hair across his chest was the queen's hair, caught in sunlight. Her body moving against his was the queen's body, pledged to another. Her eyes shining in the last light of the fire were the queen's eyes Paulus never dared to meet.

"He died out on the ice," she said when he asked, a few days later. "Hunting whales."

How long since he had had a woman? Nearly a year, Paulus thought. And he did not want to let this woman go. For her, perhaps longer. She said that her man who died hunting whales was her first, and only. The way she spoke of him made Paulus conscious that he had never felt that way about any woman but the queen, whom he could never have. The queen, with her dying husband and the seneschal Mario Tremano plotting against her. He had come to the ends of the earth, slain a dragon, to realize the futility of his desire. If he could not have her, he could at least save her. This, too, Joy had taught him. Paulus was stronger now. The time was coming when he would have to leave. The dragon's heart and eyes were almost dried. He had carefully cleaned the bits of gum and blood from its teeth, for presentation to his queen. But he was not ready to leave yet. He started obliquely, and over the early weeks of spring more directly, gauging her reactions to the idea of coming south. He described the city, the Keep on the Ridge, the queen, his brother the fool. Subtlety never came easy to him and was impossible to maintain; on the first day in May, he told her that his errand was not yet complete. He must return to The Fells.

"I would have you come with me," he said. They were tangled in a blanket and in each other's scents. Night was falling. She would never know what it had cost him to speak the words. Having Joy meant acquiescing to the caprice of Fate that kept him apart from the queen he would love. Having Joy meant being a curiosity at court, the guard captain who had once been a dog and now had a wife with callused hands from a distant land, who had never seen silk. But he was willing. He would take her if she said yes.

"I would have you stay here," Joy said. "But I know you will not. Go."

"In a little while," Paulus said.

Joy shook her head. "If you know that you are going, go," she said. "Go to your queen. Go."

"You saved my life," he said. Meaning that he felt an obligation to her, but also that he believed she too was obligated, that once she had held his life in her hands, she was no longer able to stand back from him and watch him go. Man logic, he thought. And she is lightning.

"I am from this place," Joy answered. "Someday when I am done mourning, I will take a man from the village, and there will be children in this house. I would take you if you would stay; but if you will not, go to your queen."

There was nothing to say to this. Paulus was not going to stay and Joy was not going to go. She had nursed him back to health, but she did not want him. She wanted a fisherman, a black-haired hunter of moose and caribou, a second chance at her man who had died on the ice. Not a soldier from a foreign land, entering his forty-seventh year, determined to finish a quest he had begun in honor of a woman he could never have. They both knew what it was to find solace for a little while and then reawaken into the desire for what they could never have, or never have again.

The next morning, Paulus saddled the horse and packed into its saddlebags the teeth and tail of the dragon, the scales, the heart, and the eyes. His sword and shield were broken, his armor shredded, his spear taken to hunt seals, the great sword ruined by a winter under snow. He had a thousand miles to cover with a knife and the sling, and a good horse. Mikal would be glad to see it, but not at all glad to see Paulus.

Perhaps the queen would be glad to see him. Perhaps.

Joy came out from the house with jerky and a fish. "I caught it this morning before you woke up. Your first meal when you ride away from the ocean should always be a fish," she said. Paulus thought he understood. He swung up onto the horse and did not look back as he rode south, up the hill track toward the mountains.

IV: Return

As Paulus came down the river toward The Fells, he had murder on his mind. Not a fair combat. Not the inevitable culmination of a long-simmering dispute. Murder. Somewhere in the tundra of the Mare Ultima, over a long winter of blood and fever and stillborn love, he had found it in himself to be a murderer. He had always believed that murderers were created from either a passion or a flaw of the soul. Now he understood that murderers could be the creatures of thought and planning and rationality too cold to forgive. He had left more than a broken sword and an obstinate woman along the shores of the Mare Ultima.

Few men had killed a dragon. Fewer still had been ridden by spirits while doing it. Paulus had become one of those men about whom songs could be sung. He tried not to wonder what all of it would mean once he had passed through the city gates and the story began to spread. The Fells looked as he remembered it: grey and jumbled along the inlets of the Black River, rising to the Keep that had looked over the estuary for five hundred years and more. He wondered about his brother Piero, who was not well, and he reminded himself that one of the first things he had to do was kill the seneschal who plotted against the queen. Everything in The Fells seemed like a story from the Book, heard so many times that he had come to believe it happened to him. *Once there was a man who killed a dragon . . .* He touched two fingers to his throat.

Journey there is, and there is Return
And no man may know
Whether the home he leaves will greet him again
What way the wind will blow.

This was a creed a man could live by, particularly a man with a limited reservoir of piety. Journey and return. The soldier knew this, as did anyone who ever wondered whether the touch of head to pillow would be the last thing felt in this world. Paulus was grateful for the Book. It was all he had of his mother, and all he had of religion, and in both cases it was enough.

The first thing he did was return Mikal's horse. Andrew the hostler looked up from restitching tack when Paulus dismounted at the stable gate. "You came back," he observed. "Get your dragon?"

"I did," Paulus said. "What did Mikal say about the horse?"

"Said he'd kill you, is all. Nothing to worry about."

"Good enough," Paulus said. He handed Andrew the horse's reins. Andrew clapped him on the shoulder and said, "Bring a bottle by later. Tell us a story."

"I've got some," Paulus said. Walking across the courtyard toward the guard post at the Great Door of the Keep, he thought that he might have more soon. Would he have the queen's gratitude? The king's? Piero would have been polishing his insults all winter. And Mario Tremano had no doubt spent the cold months refining his plans. This is not the place I left, Paulus thought suddenly and forcefully. He no longer knew where he stood. His old soldier's instincts prickled on the back of his neck and made his right hand jumpy.

First, then, to do what could be done easily, which was see Mikal about the horse. He reported to the guard post as if he had been away for an hour instead of nearly a year. Mikal was writing something. "We drown horse thieves around here," he said without looking up.

"By the time you've retired from the guard," Paulus said, "you'll be telling everyone you lent me the horse and it bit the dragon to death while I pissed myself."

"He goes to the Mare Ultima and comes back a jester like his brother," Mikal said to the air. Then he looked Paulus in the eye and added, "Speaking of your brother, he died a month ago."

They stayed like that, gazes locked, until Paulus knew there would be either blinking or killing. Because he would not kill Mikal, he blinked. "A month ago," he said.

"The day before the death of the king himself," Mikal said. "The queen is still in mourning. Your guess as to which of them she mourns more."

So this was how it was to live in The Fells now, Paulus thought. He left the guard post and went to keep his long-delayed appointment with the queen.

She received him in her chambers and called for wine and food. Paulus ate and drank out of politeness, feeling her gaze on him and numbering in his mind the differences she would see from the Paulus who had ridded out of The Fells nearly a year before. "We are pleased that you survived," she said after some time.

Paulus loosened the drawstring of the saddlebags he was carrying like a satchel. "I have brought the king prizes," he said. The correctness was excruciating. Accustomed to keeping his peace because he had nothing to say, Paulus grew frustrated when silence was enforced by custom and fear of transgression. He wanted to ask about his brother, but knew he would have to wait for the queen to broach the subject.

"You have not heard?" the queen said. "Our sovereign has passed. I rule in his stead, the Widow Queen of The Fells."

"I am sorry," Paulus said. "I had not heard." Nothing was to be gained by telling her the truth. "If I may serve, I hope you will tell me how."

"When a man with a sword asks me that, I begin to think I should be afraid of something that I have not yet recognized as a threat. Is that the case, Paulus?" The queen looked at him directly. Her tone was arch but there was no hint of jest in her gaze. Paulus understood: she feared being overheard.

He opened the saddlebag. "Merely the pledge of the devoted soldier, Majesty," he said. "I hope these tokens will demonstrate that devotion."

On the table next to the wine and the platter, Paulus laid out the dragon's eyes and heart and teeth. He held up one of the scales to catch the firelight. "Marvelous," the queen said. "I thank you, Paulus. The king would have been very happy." She held up one of the teeth, as long as the ceremonial dagger at the seneschal's belt. "Were you badly wounded?"

"I was fortunate," Paulus said. "The people there nursed me."

Again she looked him in the eye and again Paulus felt a near-hypnotic compulsion to tell her every secret he'd ever kept. "That is fortunate, for The Fells as well as for you," said the queen. She held the dragon's tooth out to him and he took it. "You may keep these as your reward. They would have meant much to the king, but to me they will be mementos of my grief. I have too many of those."

She had just made him rich. And if she was correct that their conversation was being overheard, she had also sent a clear signal that Paulus was one of her favorites. With perfect gentleness and delicacy, she had entrapped him in court intrigue. Willingly Paulus entered the trap. "Your generosity humbles me, Majesty," he said. "I hope to repay it."

"No doubt you shall, Paulus," the queen said. She opened the door and he walked into the corridors of the Keep a marked man, and a man with a mission. He wondered if he would have time to mourn his brother properly before the tensions of succession boiled over into killing.

When he returned to the guard post, Mikal received him as if their previous conversation had never happened. "You'll be on garrison duty until we figure out what to do with a dragon-killing hero," Mikal said. "Enjoy the rest." Paulus went to the garrison and found an empty bunk. He wanted to sleep but first he had to do something with the dragon trophies. They would be gone the minute he turned his back on them, or closed his eyes, in the garrison. Leaving his traveling gear on the bunk, he went back down to the stables, stopping along the way to wangle a bottle of wine from the kitchen steward.

"That didn't take long," Andrew observed when Paulus came into his workshop.

"Important things don't need may words," Paulus said. He uncorked the bottle and offered it to Andrew, who drank and handed it back.

When they'd passed it twice more, Paulus asked, "What happened to my brother?"

"He died," Andrew said.

"He was a young man," Paulus said.

Andrew nodded. "That he was. Sometimes young men die."

Behind Andrew's reticence Paulus sensed something else. A story that could not be told, or a lie that Andrew could not bring himself to tell. "Was he sick?" Paulus asked.

"He was himself," Andrew said. "Spitting out his jokes until the day the king died. Then he was silent for a day, and then the next morning he was dead too."

"Andrew," Paulus said. "How many other young men who were friends to the queen died after the king?"

Andrew drank, his eyes hooded and focused on something in the shadowed corners of his workshop. He looked as if he might speak but drank again instead. Finally he said, "That tomb, in the desert. How many men were buried with that king?" And would say no more.

Paulus didn't need to hear any more. He sat with Andrew, watching the wine disappear, taking a sip every so often but mostly just listening to Andrew talk. When the talking slowed, Paulus sat and waited. Andrew began to snore. Paulus left him there and went back to the barracks. He had stowed the dragon trophies in Andrew's workshop where they would be safe.

For two weeks he settled into the routines of the Keep, or tried to. Everything seemed to have changed invisibly while he was gone. He was aware of changes but not of what they were. Almost every night he woke from poorly remembered dreams and came down to Andrew's workshop. The hostler slept little and they were glad of each other's company. Paulus kept the conversation away from his brother and the queen. Soon enough he would have to deal with both, but first he let the road dust fall from his boots and the weariness of the journey abate.

On the fifteenth day after his return, when Paulus awoke in the night, he stayed with Andrew only long enough to recover the bag of trophies and toast the pregnancy of Andrew's eldest daughter. Leaving the stables, Paulus walked around to the kitchen doors at the rear of the Keep. They were barred at this hour. "Guard," he said, and knocked. A scullion, eyes puffy with sleep and onions, drew back the bar and Paulus entered. It was after midnight. The Keep's bakers were punching down their loaves and the kitchens smelled of yeast and coffee. Paulus moved among the bakers to the broad oaken doors that led to the Keep's great dining hall. They too were barred at this hour of the night. He had another scullion open them and said as he pulled them closed again, "Bar this door behind me. Let no one in."

What stories they would tell he did not know, nor whether they would connect him with what he was about to do.

Being a soldier had taught Paulus how to move silently and how to kill. Both of those skills would be of use. He was much less confident of his ability to silence an innocent without killing; this, too, he was hoping to do. He climbed the stairs that led from the rear of the dining hall up eleven floors to the top of the tower that looked along the Ridge of the Keep and down into the Jingle. At the eighth floor he left the stairwell and followed a narrow corridor that led to a catwalk ringing the inside of a part of the tower that had burned centuries ago and never been rebuilt—although the catwalk testified to a project begun and never completed. He came to a window and looked across the hundred yards of space between the tower and the central complex, the Old Keep. There, a floor below, a light burned in the chamber of Mario Tremano.

Paulus went back down to the second floor and emerged onto the roof of the kitchen. The smell of yeast surrounded him again, carried through the dozen chimneys that reached above Paulus' head. He made his way along the edge of the roof until he came to the wall of the Old Keep. There he ate a piece of the dragon's heart. It was bitter and tough, with a pungency that brought tears to his eyes, and as he swallowed it Paulus felt a bloom of strength in his limbs. The silent, darkened courtyards snapped into focus and the small noises of the night came clearly to his ears. He wedged his fingers into the gaps between the ancient stones of the keep and began to climb.

When he swung over the sill of Mario Tremano's open window, Paulus was surprised to see the seneschal seated by his hearth sipping what smelled like spiced wine. "It's not like you to skulk," Tremano said. "Have you turned assassin?"

Paulus stood at the window. "What happened to my brother?" he asked.

"You might have asked me that at any time. Why now?" Tremano drank off the rest of the wine. "My assessment of the situation is that you're not at all interested in the answer because you've already decided on my guilt. So, shall I confess? Very well. Your brother was a chaotic addition to a court that needs above all else stability. And he was sick. I did not kill him, but neither did I make sure that the physicians did everything in their power to save him. Now. What do you intend?"

"You have the logic backwards," Paulus said. "My brother died before the king."

"A man in my position does not react. He plans." Mario Tremano stood and approached Paulus. "I repeat: What do you intend?"

"I will serve my queen," Paulus said.

The seneschal shook his head and looked over Paulus' shoulder out the window. "This is not the court you left, Paulus. It would be well for you to consider that."

Paulus had come to the seneschal's chambers intending murder. He had spent much of his journey down from the Mare Ultima contemplating murder. Now, when the time for the deed was at hand, he had no stomach for it. The effects of the dragon's heart were already fading. He felt slow and thick. Brushing past Tremano, he walked toward the chamber door. The seneschal, ever courteous, accompanied him.

As Paulus put his hand on the doorknob, wrought in the shape of a dragon, he felt something drag across the underside of his jaw. He twisted away and felt the blade of a knife open the skin behind his ear. Mario Tremano, astonished, found his voice when Paulus drew his sword. "Guard!" he cried. Paulus split his skull and turned to face the guard who burst in. His name was Livio. He and Paulus had served together on a half-dozen campaigns.

Paulus pointed at the cut and the blood running down the back of his neck. "You see what happened, Livio," he said.

"I'm not sure what I see," Livio said. "But Mikal will need to see it as well."

"Don't," Paulus said. There were voices in the hall, footsteps on the stairs; Mario Tremano's shout had roused this part of the Keep.

"You can't kill the seneschal and walk away, Paulus," Livio said. His sword point lowered.

"No," Paulus said. "I doubt I can." Then he punched Livio in the head with his sword hand. Livio reeled and Paulus threw him to the floor. He ran out of the seneschal's chamber, deflected a surprised sword thrust from a guardsman coming down the corridor, and kept running until he came to the gates of the Keep. "An errand from the queen," he panted at the gatekeeper. Behind him, the outcry was growing. "Now!" Paulus demanded. "I must pass."

The gatekeeper hesitated.

"The queen commands it!" Paulus said.

The gatekeeper raised the bar and Paulus shoved through. In the courtyard voices were crying murder and shouting his name. He ran again, through the mazy streets of The Fells, tearing off his guard tunic along the way and arriving in Nightside Jingle winded, desperate, and certain that he would never pass alive through the gates of the Keep again. Nightside Jingle was the midnight twin of the market, a bazaar whose staple commodities were sex and killing. It was a good place to hide.

Hiding turned into living somehow. No parties from the Keep came to hunt him down, and Paulus assumed that the queen's last favor to him was this unspoken amnesty. He hired out his sword when he could, and when he could not, he sold off bits of the dragon: a scale here, a tooth there.

It was in one of those hungry periods, a year after he had killed Mario Tremano, that Paulus first met the men of the Agate Tower.

V: THE AGATE TOWER

It speared up into the sky from a ridge southwest of the Keep, twice as tall as any other building in The Fells. No one knew by what means it had been erected, or whether it had always been a house of wizards. What went into the Agate Tower rarely came out unless it had been transformed first. That was true of its apprentices, certainly, but less often of certain prominent citizens who went to the wizards looking for something that the brokers down by the river could not sell them, some magic more powerful than could be cobbled together from the bartered essences of fishmongers and orphans. The wizards who lived within took on apprentices rarely, giving no reasons for their choices. They worked magic for money, but also sometimes—as they termed it—"for Law," which meant acts of magic performed to restore imbalances created by brokered magics. By and large the wizards were monkish, living out their lives within the walls of the Tower unless drawn out into The Fells or the wider world on some errand for guild or sovereign. No one trusted wizards.

Paulus, hating magic, avoided the Agate Tower and the stretch of winding, mossy streets that surrounded it. He kept to the other end of town, the Jingle and the Nightside and the downriver districts, unless work brought him upstream to the richer areas. But even for a merchant's money, Paulus wouldn't go to the Agate Tower. Magic, as far as he could see, had never done a good thing for him in his life. It gave short-term relief from long-term problems.

"For a man who hates magic, you seem to draw it," commented a stranger one night in a pub called simply the Fish, where Paulus was sharing stories the way lonely men did when wine loosened their tongues.

"True," Paulus said.

"You've killed a dragon and a seneschal, and here you are drinking the last of your coins and hoping that the morning will bring another chance to kill for a living," the stranger said. "That's uncommon."

Paulus took a closer look at the stranger. He was a young man, his face unscarred and a dove-gray leather glove on his right hand. He wore a ring over the glove on the middle finger of that hand. An apprentice of the Tower.

The conversation took on a different meaning. The apprentice saw Paulus register the ring and the glove. "You need work, or so we have heard," he said. "The Tower could use a man with your qualities."

"Qualities," Paulus repeated.

"You survived the ghost and its geas. That alone puts you in a very small company," the apprentice said. "The geas itself would have left hoof marks all over the minds of most men. And then there's your older story."

"Don't," Paulus said. He hadn't told that story tonight, or ever in the Fish. "If you say the word *dog* there's going to be blood."

Unruffled, the apprentice went on. "I hear you've been trying to sell some bits of dragon. What do you have left?"

"Are you buying?" Paulus asked.

"The Tower is buying. We'll buy your dragon bits, and we'd like to make an offer on you as well."

Paulus had found it difficult to move the dragon's teeth and scales because he could not prove their authenticity without resorting to revealing who he was and therefore possibly letting news of his whereabouts filter back to the Keep. The eyes and heart were trickier still, because they were rare enough to be worth enormous amounts of money, and few people rich enough to part with that much money were gullible enough to do it without being certain of what they were getting.

The queen, in giving Paulus the trophies from the dragon, had made him rich in a currency that was nearly impossible to spend.

"An offer on me," Paulus said. "For what?"

"To do the kind of thing you do," the apprentice said. With a self-mocking conjuror's flourish, he produced an inch-high column of gold coins from his sleeve. "Take this as a token of earnestness. We will see you tomorrow at midday if you wish to know more."

The apprentice left. The other patrons of the Fish eyed Paulus' new wealth. He called out to the barkeep and circled his finger over his head. "One for the house," he said.

When he went to the Tower the next day, Paulus began to learn that its mysteries were both unyielding and uninteresting. The wizards did what they did according to protocols that were their protocols. He did not have to learn them and did not want to. The first day, they purchased from him the teeth and scales and the remainder of the heart. Paulus used the money to buy a good horse and take a room over a public house on a steep hill near the Jingle. At first he dealt with Eyler, the young apprentice who had come seeking him in the Fish. The wizards desire that you should travel to thus-and-such a place to bring back this or that article, Eyler would say, and Paulus would go and do it. He had in his possession, briefly, strange artifacts of vanished races and scrolls in languages that looked like mathematics. To gather them he rode to some of the cities he had previously seen as a soldier: Ie Fure, Averon, Muska. Most of these journeys were uneventful; on those occasions when he was called upon to fight, Paulus fought without relish, as a professional does.

At other times he escorted one of the Tower's wizards to a library or ruin, or a gathering of wizards from different cities where they disputed points of what they called the Law. Paulus gathered that this Law had something to do with the matter of the universe. He inquired no further and his waking hours were untroubled. When he awoke in the night, however, he realized that the atmosphere of the Agate Tower, the forces that gathered and swirled there, had permeated him somehow. Eyler had been right; he did draw magic. Its echoes sounded in the chambers of his heart. Paulus began to dream badly.

A year and a half after Paulus entered the employ of the Tower, Eyler took off his glove and entered the society of wizards. Shortly after, Paulus found Eyler in the Tower's library. "You were right," he said. "I draw magic. Why?"

"Not an easy question," Eyler said.

"If it was an easy question, I wouldn't need a wizard to answer it."

"Think of how often magic has been worked on you," Eyler said. "The ghost of the king. The geas. The transformation. Most men who are transformed into animals lose parts of their minds when their human form is restored. You did not. And you survived the ghost, and you have eaten of the heart of a dragon and felt a dragon's blood on your skin. You are saturated in echoes and aftereffects and traces. Like draws like; how could the magic in this tower not find you?"

Paulus imagined himself trailing wisps of magic wherever he went. He imagined magic creeping and battening upon his body and soul. For the first time he understood that magic was not always something that someone did; it simply was. He had made himself vulnerable to it.

"I sleep badly," he said to Eyler. "And my dreams are hard."

"Ah, dreams. When the mind and spirit move from sleeping to waking . . . that is a Journey and a Return, is it not? The journey is dangerous and the return is never to the place that was left. Magic inhabits and animates the same space where dreams occur," Eyler said. "At least that is what we have learned so far. So a man like you, with the tracks of so much magic on you, will feel his dreams drawn to the memories of that magic. How could it be otherwise?"

"That's what I was going to ask you," Paulus said.

The dreams went on: Paulus on the floor of the throne room, eyes closed, breathing in rhythm to the quiet snoring of the king. His brother turning handsprings and composing witty couplets about courtiers' bedroom peccadilloes. The gentle touch of the queen, falling away as Paulus rose to walk on two legs again. The silence of the tomb, and the ghost burrowed away like a worm in his mind, its twisting track left behind even after the broker boiled it down to an essence that a desperate man could pour over a sword and use to kill a dragon. The stink of his fear and the dragon's blood.

Joy.

He awoke in the hours before dawn, sometime in midsummer. All gone. All the matter of Paulus' life, gone. Remaining only as something to mourn. Paulus rose and walked out into The Fells. There was one man living who would understand. He came to the stable gate in the shadow of the Keep's walls. "Andrew," he said to the stableboy who answered his knock. A short while later the hostler appeared. He looked over his shoulder, then back at Paulus. "If you're going to risk your life, I hope you at least brought a bottle," he said.

Paulus followed him into the workshop. He had heard little of what went on inside the Keep since leaving it. Andrew caught him up and it became clear to Paulus that nothing had changed in three years. Mario Tremano was dead, but the falling of that tree let other treacherous saplings find sunlight. The queen was strong, Andrew said, but the court still struggled with the consequences of the king's death and Tremano's scheming. There was talk that a war might be necessary to paper over divisions among the nobility. Listening, Paulus was struck by how little any of it mattered. The queen was strong? Good. Enough. Let the rest of it happen how it would.

"I thought once that I might be able to see her again," he said.

Andrew shook his head. "You'd be forcing her to make an example of you. As much as she loved you, that wouldn't stop her. Things end, Paulus. You've got to let them end. Especially when you're the one who ended them."

The bottle passed between them. Light began to show through the workshop's shuttered windows. "You'd better go before it gets light," Andrew said. "It was good to see you, old friend. Don't come again."

Paulus went out into the dawn. He had meant to ask Andrew a question but the time had never been quite right and now, coming down the Ridge of the Keep toward the river, he knew that the point of the visit had not been to ask the question but to learn that he would always have provided his own answer no matter what Andrew said. He had made a farewell.

VI: The Price of Forgetting

Too many lives tangled his mind. Too many losses kept his heart broken. Paulus realized that he could not stand to be himself any more and there was only one thing he could think of to do. He walked all day through The Fells, calculating. Things should have been different, he thought. But they were as they were. In the afternoon he made a final decision and returned to the quayside block where the spell brokers mixed and tinctured their perilous wares. He stopped outside the shop where he had killed Jan Destrier before leaving on his errand to kill the dragon. Another broker had moved in, probably while Destrier's body was still warm and Paulus' horse had not yet broken a sweat. But that was in the past.

I might have stayed with Joy, Paulus thought. I might have refused to be the queen's instrument. I might have chosen a less foolish way to attempt to avenge my father.

He could see that he had been fortunate in ways that most men had not. Still, his peculiar fortunes had brought him sadness. Luck was not always lucky. Loyalty had brought him no peace.

He entered the broker's shop. The man behind the table was not Jan Destrier, of course, but he might as well have been. Fashions among the spell brokers were oddly dictatorial. They all seemed to be fat men wearing too many rings and cut stones in their beards. "What do you seek?" the broker asked.

"I want to forget," Paulus said.

"What do you want to forget?" The broker pared his nails. "Every man has something he wants to forget. If you purchase carelessly, you might forget more than you had wished."

"I want to forget the dragon. My brother Piero. And her." Paulus stood, and waited. "No. Not Piero."

"Maybe you should make up your mind," the broker said.

"Maybe you should keep your mouth shut and your hands busy," Paulus said. He did not look at the broker. He waited until a phial appeared on the tabletop in front of him.

"There will be a cost," the broker said.

"I know."

"Specificity brings a greater cost."

"I will pay," Paulus said. From the pouch at his belt he brought forth the dragon's eyes. "There is more. I will pay. Tell me what."

VII: Wizard's Six

In the spring Paulus set out north from The Fells, hunting the apprentice Myros. He cannot be allowed to collect his six, the wizard had said. If you cannot find his track, you must kill whichever of the six he has already selected. It did Paulus' conscience no good to kill people whose only fault was being collected by an aspiring wizard, but he would be only the first of many hunters. Without the guild's protection, a wizard's six were like baby turtles struggling toward the sea. Best to spare them a life of being hunted.

The apprentice had spent enough time in the Agate Tower to know that there would be pursuit. He was moving fast and had four months' head start; Paulus moved faster, riding through nights and spring storms, fording spring-swollen rivers, asking quiet questions over bottles in public houses along the only road over the mountains. He killed the first of the apprentice's collection on a farm between a bend in the road and a ripple of foothills: a small boy with a dirty face and a stick in his hand.

Yes, mister, a man passed by here in the winter.

Yes, mister, he had a ring over his glove. I was feeding the pig, and he told me I was a likely boy. Are you looking for him?

Can I see your sword?

They weren't supposed to choose children, Paulus was thinking as he rode on. Even apart from the cultural sanction, children's magic was powerful but unpredictable, tricky to harness. No wonder the guild was after this one.

In a public house that evening, the day's chill slowly ebbing from his feet, Paulus said a prayer for the boy's parents. He hoped they hadn't sent anyone after him. It was bad enough to kill children; he had even less desire to take the lives of vengeful bumpkins. Best to keep moving. Already he had gained a month on the apprentice, who was moving fast for a normal man but not fast enough to stay ahead of Paulus, who had once been one of the king's rangers. Upstairs in his room, Paulus watched a thin drift of snow appear on the windowsill, spilling onto the plank floor. His prayer beads worked through his fingers. Go, boy, he thought. Speed your way to heaven. He dreamed of turtles, and of great birds that flew at night.

In the morning the snow had stopped, and Paulus cut a piece of cheese from a wheel left out in the kitchen. He stuck the knife in the remaining cheese and set a coin next to it, then left through the back door and saddled his horse without waking the stable boy. He rode hard, into the mountains and over the first of the passes where the road lay under drifted snow taller than a man on horseback. The horse picked out the track; like Paulus, it had been this way before. It was blowing hard by noon, when they had come to the bottom of a broad valley dotted with farms and a single manor house. Paulus rode to the gates of the manor and waited to be noticed.

The gate creaked open, revealing a choleric elder in threadbare velvet, huddled under a bearskin cloak. "Who comes to the house of Baron Branchefort?"

Paulus dismounted and let the seneschal see the sigil of the Agate Tower dangling from the horse's bridle. "I ride on an errand from the wizards' guild in The Fells," he said. "Has an apprentice traveled through this valley?"

"And how would I know an apprentice?"

"He would wear a ring over the glove on his right hand. He is called Myros."

The elder nodded. "Aye, he was here. Visited the Baron asking permission to gather plant lore."

"Was this granted?"

"It was. He was our guest for a week and a day, then rode to the head of the valley."

"Did he gather any herbs?"

"I did not observe."

"You wouldn't have. His errand has nothing to do with plants. He travels to collect children."

The elder held Paulus' gaze for a long moment. "This is why you follow him."

"It is. Are there children in your house?"

"No. The Baron nears his eightieth year. We have few servants, and no children."

Paulus offered up a prayer of thanks that he would not have to enter the manor. He had seen more than enough of noble houses fallen into somnolence. Standing at the gate of this one, his chest constricted and he thought of his brother.

"Where," he asked, "are the houses in this valley with children?"

The elder looked up at the sky, then down at the ground between his feet. "Many children come into this world," he said. "Few survive. Only one of the Baron's vassals has children below marriageable age. He is called Philo, and his house is the last before the road rises into the mountains again."

Paulus nodded and mounted his horse again.

"You will ease Philo's mind, I pray," the elder said.

"What ease I can give, I will give," Paulus said, and rode north.

Philo's house lay in the shadow of a double peak, across the saddle of which lay Paulus' route over the mountains. As Paulus rode up, the sun rested between the peaks. A man about Paulus' age, but with the caved-in chest and stooped neck of too much work and not enough food, was drawing water. A girl of seven or eight years stood waiting with an empty bucket.

"Philo," Paulus said.

"That is my name," Philo said, without looking up at Paulus, as he hauled a full bucket over the edge of the well. He emptied it into the bucket his daughter set on the ground at his feet. "And this is my daughter Sophia. Now you know what of us is worth knowing."

"A young man wearing a ring over his glove has been here," Paulus said.

Philo dropped the bucket back into the well. "He has."

"He spoke to your daughter."

"That's right, sir, he did. Told her she was a likely girl. She's always seemed so to me, but if I was any judge of men or girls I wouldn't be here." Still Philo had not met Paulus' gaze. Paulus began to wonder what had passed between him and Myros; or was his demeanor caused by the Brancheforts?

No matter.

"I come from The Fells," Paulus said. "My instructions are to gather the girl he spoke to. For service at the Agate Tower."

At this, Philo looked up and Paulus and put a hand around his daughter's thin shoulders. Now it was Paulus who wanted to look away. He forced himself to hold Philo's eye. "She's my only, sir," Philo said. "And my wife, we're too old to have another."

"Philo," Paulus said. "I have no quarrel with you. My errand is my errand."

He watched the awful calculus of the peasant on Philo's face. One fewer mouth to feed. Giving his daughter over to a life of service with the wizards of The Fells, where she would spend the rest of her days forgetting what it was like to go to bed hungry. And against that . . .

"May we visit her, sir?"

"When she has been gone a year," Paulus said. He was a poor liar, but this provision he remembered from his own journey to The Fells as a boy, when he had been taken into the King's Acrobats.

His mother had never come. After a year he had stopped expecting her.

"Before that," he said, "she will still long for home. You may write as long as you do not ask her to return. Censors at the guild will destroy your letters if you do."

Philo was nodding slowly. "We do love her, sir," he said. "She's our only."

And through all this, the girl Sophia spoke not a word.

"I will return in the morning," Paulus said.

The ruse had cost him a day, and cost him, too, any chance of a better meal than jerky eaten under a tree. Paulus had started back to the manor house, then veered away from the road into a copse of beech and spruce. He had already lied more that day than during the previous ten years, and could no more maintain his fabrications than strike down young Sophia of Branchefort Valley in her father's presence. So he hobbled his horse, found dry ground beneath the spreading branches of a spruce tree, and prayed until sleep came. Then he dreamed of his mother, refusing to look at him as he craned his neck to see through the wagon gate and cried out *Mama, goodbye, Mama.*

In the morning, Sophia was waiting in the lambskin coat Philo had been wearing the afternoon before. Rabbit fur wrapped her feet, and she held a small satchel in both hands. Philo and her mother stood behind her, each with a hand on her; the woman's hand moved to smooth the coat's collar, tug a tangle out of Sophia's hair. Philo reached down and took his daughter's hand.

"May she write us?" the woman said.

"After a year, ma'am," answered Paulus. "Should she prove unsuitable, I will bring her back myself, with no dishonor to you. It's many a child isn't meant for the wizards' service."

"Not unsuitable, not our Sophia," Philo said. He swallowed.

"Philo," Paulus said. "Can you spare this coat? She will be warm on the journey."

"I'd like her to have it," Philo said. "It's all we can give her."

Paulus could come up with no convincing reply. "There's fresh eggs and bread in the bag," Sophia's mother said.

"I thank you, ma'am," Paulus said. "I am Paulus. Your man and I met yesterday."

"I am Clio, sir," she said. She was looking hard at him—seeing, Paulus knew, the scars on his hands and the long sword on his right hip.

"Your daughter has her destiny, Clio," Paulus said. "I am here to take her to it."

Baby turtles, he told himself. Another might have killed all three by now, and moved on. The thought gave him no ease. He averted his eyes as Philo and Clio made their farewells. Braver than either, Sophia took Paulus' hand and climbed onto the saddle in front of him. A tremor ran through her small body, but she reached out to get her fists into the horse's mane. She looked back at her parents as Paulus spurred the horse northward, and he wondered what she saw.

When she spoke, much later when the northern pass out of Branchefort Valley was behind them, Paulus didn't register her voice at first. He was thinking about the boy who had been feeding his pig when Myros came. How easily children died. "Sir?" the girl said. "What do you call the horse?"

"I never named him," Paulus said.

"Can I call him Brown?"

"All right."

"Your name is Brown," Sophia told the horse.

He could kill her at any time, could have killed her at any moment since crossing the pass. Could, for that matter, have cut her down with the empty bucket in her hands while her father was drawing water. Hesitation kills, Paulus thought.

"What are the wizards like?" she asked.

"They are wizards," Paulus said. "Not like men. But not cruel."

"How long until we get there?"

"A little while yet," Paulus said. He was silent after that, and they rode the edge of a canyon in which night fell early and forced them to make camp while the sky above was still light.

At times, Paulus knew, he was slow to apprehend the consequences of his actions. Now he realized that he had complicated his task first by concocting a story and then by taking the girl. She was one of the apprentice's six; Myros might well know that Paulus had her, and if he also knew about the boy he might be provoked into retaliation. Better to have killed her quickly and ridden on. Regardless of the wizard's injunction, Paulus could not afford to carry her with him in his pursuit of Myros. Nor could he return her, now that his mouth had run away with his reason and pronounced that she might be returned if she did not satisfy the wizards. He could easily imagine what such a stigma might mean to a child in a place like Branchefort Valley. He stirred Philo's eggs over the fire and damned himself for losing sight of his task.

Over the sound of the night breeze in the canyon, he heard Sophia crying quietly. End this, he thought, and rose into a crouch.

"I'm afraid," she said, and the sound of her voice destroyed his resolve. He sat next to her. Paulus had no knowledge of children. He had none of his own and had been taken from his own home at about Sophia's age, leaving behind three younger sisters whom he had never seen again.

"Never been out of the valley before?" he asked her.

She shook her head and wiped at her nose before tearing a piece of bread from the loaf and scooping eggs out of the bowl. Cowardice was a thick, bitter syrup in Paulus' throat. The boy with the stick in his hand had fallen without a sound, face still bearing traces of his smile at seeing Paulus' sword—yet Paulus knew that in the dying reaches of the boy's brain had been the knowledge of his murder. He found that he could not bear the idea of Sophia dying with that same knowledge. Her name, he thought. If I had not learned her name . . .

"Let me tell you a story," Paulus said, and then he fell silent because he couldn't remember any stories. He remembered the sound of his father's voice telling him stories when he was a small boy, but he couldn't hear any of the words. "There was a little girl who dreamed that she was a bird," he began, and he let his voice follow the idea of that bird until Sophia was asleep. In the morning he buried the crusts of the bread with her, and burned the coat over her grave. As he climbed out of the canyon into sunlight, a wind sharp with snow raised gooseflesh on his arms. He filled his lungs and held his breath until the edges of his vision faded into red, then exhaled slowly, slowly, feeling his mind start to fade. At the point of unconsciousness he let himself breathe again, deeply and freely. He did not remember where he had learned the exercise, but it cleared his mind, and as his horse—Brown—picked his way across frosted scree below a peak like the head of a boil, Paulus let his mind wander. During the short time he had slept the night before, he had dreamed of being a dog, in a warm room with thick rugs and two great stone chairs too high for him to leap onto. There had been a kind woman and an old, old man, and another man who would not look at him but spoke gently. *O queen*, he thought; and after that, *O brother*.

The motion of a hare bounding between rocks drew his attention. He slipped an old throwing knife from its sheath at the small of his back and waited for it to move again, thinking that now he was over the first high ridge of peaks and in this expanse of alpine valleys, game would be more plentiful. In the high country, above treeline, was nothing but pikas and the occasional adventuresome goat. He wished he had brought a bow, but the truth was that no one had ever mistaken him for a skillful archer; his boyhood circus training, though, had served him well where knives were concerned. When the hare made its move, Paulus flicked his wrist. Simple. Five minutes later, the hare was dressed and dangling from his saddle. He rode on, trying not to think of sopping up the hare's fat with Sophia's bread. Skill with knives or no, Paulus knew that hunger was going to be a close companion as he moved farther from settled regions. The hermits and occasional isolated hamlets huddled in the valleys would not all be as hospitable as the Brancheforts had been.

Sparser settlement also meant that it would be harder to track Myros—although Myros would have his own problems, chief among them finding four more children to collect. Paulus had no doubt that all six of Myros' collection would be children, and the certainty had come so quietly that he was reluctant to examine it too closely. He mistrusted his own intuition, feeling that it was often fueled by whatever it was he had paid the wizard to make him forget, and he feared breaking the spell by looking too closely at the workings of his mind.

There was the problem, too, of where Myros was going—and why. Moving north as fast as feet could carry him, moving deeper and deeper into the winter that had already left the lowlands, Myros fled as if frantic to go backwards in time. If he kept heading north, he would reach the marshes and tundras that gave onto the ice-choked Mare Ultima. What would Myros want with the tribes who followed the whales and caribou?

A stirring in Paulus' mind set his fingers tingling with more than the cold. *I can block the memories of your mind*, the broker had said, *but the body's memories are beyond my reach.* Paulus looked at his hands and wondered what they remembered. He had paid good silver for his forgetfulness, but no wizard had yet charmed the curiosity out of man or woman, or the desire. Paulus' brother was ample evidence of that.

VIII: The Lesson

Days passed, and fell from memory with the sunset. Paulus saw no one, and stopped remembering his dreams. He was well into the second range of mountains, leading Brown on a foot trail skirting snow-buried canyons, when he found the apprentice's third. He saw smoke funneling out of a crevice on the canyon wall, and found a cave entrance below it. Calling in, he roused an old hermit and described Myros. "Yes," the hermit nodded, and invited Paulus in for hot water and flat bread. "He was here. And yes, he spoke to my lad and moved on. Quite a soft one to be this deep in the mountains."

Paulus thought, but did not say, that there were many kinds of hardness.

"And he would not eat, nor drink," the hermit went on. Paulus watched his fingers, how they moved through the silent catechism of the hermit's god. Nine beads on a catgut string, a sacred abacus ticking off the arithmetic of holiness. I will pray after, Paulus thought. Not now.

"I thank you for your welcome," he said.

The hermit did not acknowledge this. "Wizards," he grumbled, and spat into the fire.

"Myros is not yet a wizard," Paulus said. "I am sent to make sure he never will be."

In the hermit's eyes, Paulus saw suspicion. And something else; their expression teased at a memory, irritating like a hair on the back of the tongue. Eyes like gray stones, they put him in mind of something, stirred echoes of a kind of love that he could not remember feeling since he was a boy.

"If you are following him," the hermit said, "what does it matter whether he spoke to my lad?"

You have not been gone from inhabited places as long as all that, old man, thought Paulus. "I need to know if he is collecting," he said, and might have said more but the hermit threw hot water in his face and at the same time someone caught hold of his hair from behind. He threw a forearm across his throat and felt the impact of the blade, and then burning as the hermit kicked the embers of the fire across his leggings. Paulus scissored his legs, scattering the coals back toward the hermit, and with his left hand gripped the wrist of whoever had hold of his hair. The blade caught him on the cheek, and with an animal roar he squeezed until he felt bones snap. The grip on his hair loosened, and he pivoted to his feet, twisting the arm and breaking it again before he saw that he held a long-haired boy of perhaps thirteen, face twisted with hate and fear and pain. Paulus let him go, and the boy sprang up with the knife again. Stepping to his right, Paulus slapped the knife hand down and punched the boy hard on the left temple, knocking him straight down into the packed-earth floor, where he laid motionless save for a slow movement of his lips.

Looking over his shoulder, Paulus saw the hermit brandishing a burning branch. I have tried lies, and I have tried truth, he thought. This time he did not speak at all.

The next morning, in the sunny mouth of a snow cave near a frozen creek, Paulus ran his fingers carefully along his wounds. He had done this the night before, but could not credit what his fingertips reported. His cheek was unmarked, though his tongue felt a chipped molar where the thrust of the boy's blade had landed, and on his forearm a deep cut ran for three inches or so, then stopped for slightly more, then began again before tapering into a scratch near the outside of his elbow. Paulus probed the skin between the two cuts as he reconstructed the fight in his mind. One blow across the arm, one blow to the cheek, then he had turned. Could he have forgotten a third strike? It seemed impossible. The uncut skin felt normal to the touch, but when he pressed the point of a knife into it, he could not leave a mark. An odd smell filled his nostrils, raising the hair on his forearms and shrinking his testicles though he could not identify it and did not know why he should be afraid. The forgetting, he thought. Perhaps the body cannot forget any more than a bird can forget to fly south.

Well. Put it from your mind, he told himself. You paid for the forgetting, and must have had a good reason.

More important was the fact that Myros knew he was being pursued. The hermit's ambush made that clear, and that meant that at the time Paulus had killed the boy on the farm, Myros had not yet collected the hermit's acolyte. So, Paulus reasoned, I am closing on him, but he will have laid traps where time and circumstances allow. Hesitation kills, and even more fatal is the failure to learn from mistakes. Three of Myros' collection remained. Each, no doubt, would pose more risk than the last—and Myros himself could not be underestimated. The time for a budding wizard to gather his collection came near the end of his studies, when he could go no further without the actual performance of magic. Together, the sparks of magic in each of the six merged into a wizard's strength, and in fact his life, since a wizard lived only as long as one of his collection survived. Paulus wasn't sure which would be more difficult, eliminating the six or confronting Myros after he had completed his collection. The apprentice would not have completed his studies, but he would have learned enough in the Agate Tower to be a difficult opponent.

Paulus had killed wizards before. He could do it again. He could also fail, and although he did not fear death, he feared dying and believed that knowledge of the difference between the two was the true wellspring of courage. Having taken money from the wizards' guild, however, Paulus knew better than to abandon his mission. He finished the flat bread he had taken from the hermit's cave, and gnawed the last of the rabbit, and went on.

◆ ◆ ◆

He came to tundra, and found a thin track that followed the course of a north-flowing river. Memories threatened, and Paulus held his breath until they went away. Five days he walked, eating little and haunted by the prospect of remembering. Often he thought of his brother, dead these four years, and of the strange sacrifice his brother had made. More often still he thought of the king whose father had killed Paulus' father, and who had taken Paulus into his service and transformed him from an acrobat into the man he now was. Something slippery and vast remained just out of reach in his mind, and although he fought the impulse he could not help grasping after it. Nor could he help tracking his fingers across the blank patch of skin between the two healing cuts, or the bearded cheek that had not parted for the acolyte's dagger. The magic is faltering, he thought, and was glad that he might be whole again but afraid that he might find his failures more complete as well.

A village of thatched huts hugged the sandy inside of a bend in the river. Four men came out to meet him, careful not to point their spears too directly at him, and speaking a language that Paulus knew only in fragments from fellow soldiers. They recognized the sigil of the king on the hilt of his sword, and the figure of the Agate Tower on the medallion tied to Brown's bridle, and when he asked about the apprentice who wore a ring over his glove they nodded and pointed to a lean-to of driftwood and sod downstream of the village.

When he knocked at the crooked sticks of the door, it fell in, and before Paulus could draw his sword he was set upon by dogs. A ringing rose in his ears and he killed them, one at a time while the others tore at his legs and leapt snarling at his face. Before they were all dead a spear struck a glancing blow across the back of his head; Paulus caught the last dog, ran it through, and used its body as a shield to catch the thrust of the next spear. He twisted the dog's body, jerking the spear from the hands of the villager who had held it, and killed him. The other three spread into a semicircle around him. Blood warm on the back of his neck, Paulus said, "He was dead when Myros came here and you did not set your dogs on him. Where is he?"

The answer was three spears, driven at once toward his gut. He stepped to his left, between two of them, and struck down the two villagers before they could regain their balance. "You're not killing caribou now," Paulus said to the last of them. "Leave off."

It wasn't working. Paulus looked into the last man's face and saw a look he had come to know well in his days with the king's army. May I never come to the point, he prayed, when I am willing to die for the sake of not being shamed by my failure to kill myself uselessly. A shouting pierced the ringing in his ears, and he looked to his left, upstream, where an old man and a younger woman stood with two children, a boy and a girl. Naked. Twins. The children stared wide-eyed at Paulus, streaked in blood and holding the carcass of a dog. They stared at the three dead men sprawled around him, and at the dead dogs fanning out from the open doorway of the driftwood lean-to. Their expressions did not change as the elder, standing behind them and looking Paulus in the eye, held up a bone knife and cut their throats before the eyes of the village. First the girl, then the boy, knelt and looked down at the blood running down their bellies. They put their hands over their wounds. The boy coughed, and sucked in a huge breath before choking blood out of his mouth. The girl's mouth opened and her tongue came out as if she had tasted something bad. Then both of them, almost at once, put out a bloody hand to the ground and used it to guide their bodies down to rest.

Something broke inside Paulus. The ringing in his ears disappeared, and he lowered his sword. "They were dead when Myros came," he repeated. "I am made the instrument of his madness."

In the woman's eyes was something neither pity nor hate. "Go," the woman said.

Many children I have let live, Paulus thought that night. Other men might have killed them all.

And still other men, he answered himself, would have returned the wizards' money before killing the boy with the stick.

Again he grasped after the easy justification: Once Myros collected them, they were going to die. Baby turtles. Paulus had been kinder about it than most would have. Still and yet, there were men who made their way in the world without killing children. Paulus prayed to one day be among them.

One more. He lay looking at the northern stars, knowing that some baby turtles survived, and thinking: One more.

And on into the country of stone and smoke and ice, where men ate seals and great bears ate men. The world is running out of land, Paulus thought. The sixth cannot be far. After the hermit's trap and the ambush laid at the village, he was no longer traveling, but patrolling, eyes and ears sharpened for possible threats, right hand moving restlessly back and forth between Brown's saddle horn and the pommel of his sword. He caught himself praying under his breath, and wondered with wry humor if this was what it took for him to discover piety. Also he had the feeling that the membrane of his forgetting was growing dangerously thin, as if the part of his mind veiled by magic was speaking to him, more loudly and insistently with each hour he traveled north.

I have been here before, he thought—and held his breath until the world grew purplish at the edges and he felt himself swaying in the saddle.

On a morning sharp with ocean breeze and the smells of northern plants awakening to the promise of summer's endless days, Paulus came upon a farmer plowing. Pulling his own blade, the man bent to his work, shirtless and running with sweat even in the chill air. Paulus rode to him, sword drawn and leveled. When the farmer looked up, he asked, "Has a young man with a ring over his glove passed this way?"

The farmer let the handles of his plow drop and squinted up at Paulus. "It's you," he said.

Paulus raised his sword, and would have killed the farmer except the man spoke his name. "How do you know my name?" he asked. "Was it Myros who told you?"

"Do you—it hasn't been that long."

"Since what?"

The farmer cocked his head. "You don't remember me, either, do you? Will?"

"Why would I?"

"Oh," the farmer—Will—said. "You had a magic done, didn't you?"

Paulus' sword point dipped in Will's direction.

"Paulus," Will said. "Your apprentice was here, yesterday, and he did collect a boy. But there's more you need to know."

"No, there isn't," Paulus said. "I don't know how you know me, or if you know me or if Myros left you this part to play. None of that matters. Take me to the boy."

"Well, I was going to do that," Will said. "After all, he's yours."

The membrane stretched thinner, and then Will added, "From Joy. When you came to kill the dragon."

And Paulus remembered.

When he tried to sleep, he heard the dragon.

The whisper of its scales, their soft scrape and rattle. The cold draft of its indrawn breath, so like the breath of a cave. The slow creak of its wings, unfolding in the dark. All memory now, the ghost of his bitter triumph scratching its way through the inside of his mind.

He rolled over, felt the mattress under him: so soft, softer than the wintry mountainside where he'd camped the night before he'd gone into the dragon's lair. In a corner of his chamber, a mouse scampered. There were hours yet before dawn.

He threw back the sheet and stood. In the courtyard below his window, the bucket hung over the well swung in the night wind. A light shone in the stables, and Paulus shrugged into a robe. The groom, Andrew, rarely slept and had grown accustomed to Paulus' intrusions in the middle of the night.

Before going down to the stables, Paulus rummaged in the dark for the bottle on his nightstand. Better to bring a gift when interrupting another man's solitude.

Andrew looked up at the squeak of the stable door's hinges. "Paulus," he said. Paulus set the bottle on the square table Andrew used to cut tack, and the old groom grinned. "The dragon again," he said.

Paulus sat heavily on the cutting bench.

Killing the dragon: the shock of the blade driven at an angle below the scales behind its shoulder, the scalding spray of blood over his hands and face (no blade can cut his face now, nor a long irregular patch of skin on the inside of his right forearm where the seam of his jerkin had split), the long ropes of skin and muscle hanging from Paulus' flanks and legs where its claws had raked him, the sight of his own bones. And then the woman who put him on a sledge and dragged him to her hearth, where the winter passed into spring without him remembering, and in the spring when he was strong again he desired her, and would have taken her back to The Fells; but although she gave freely of her body and her love, she would not leave her birthplace. So he had come back, and slept little and drunk much, and spent the dying hours of the night with Andrew at the tack bench, until with the last of the bounty on the dragon he had purchased his forgetting.

Paulus woke.

In her language, her name meant Joy. She had had one man before him, killed the year before hunting the horned whales among the ice floes of the Mare Ultima. Perhaps she had had none after.

He could remember the smell of the cutting bench as if it were in the room with him. The morning after sharing that last bottle with Andrew, he had gone to a spell broker and negotiated the terms of his forgetting. Now he remembered it all again: The pain that crept like worms under his skin as the dragon's poison did its slow work, the way the screams had fought their way out of his mouth as she dragged him down the hillside and for miles along the riverside trail. The pungency of her remedies, and the spasms of his body as they drew the poisons out. The long silences in her house, broken only by the whickering of the wind in the thatched roof—and at last the moment when he had caught her hand and said, *Come to me.*

The boy, Paulus thought. The boy now sleeping on his pallet near the farmer's hearth. He could be mine.

I want him to be mine.

He could never have imagined himself feeling this. He felt newly full, spilling over, as if the unstoppering of his memory had scoured away other walls. Paulus sat up, sealskin covers falling away from him. He had spoken to the boy the day before, Will hanging back with more discretion than Paulus would have expected. A simple conversation, and when the boy had asked in his pidgin four-year-old way to see Paulus' sword, Paulus knew he did not have it in him to kill this boy. Perhaps it was the fact that he might be killing his own offspring—though that had not stopped a number of men Paulus had known, and even admired—and perhaps it was simply the lesson of this journey. The Book of the god to whom Paulus prayed spoke of the Journey, and the Lesson. Part of Paulus' attraction to this faith was his life's own journeying, the travels and travails; now here was a chapter of the Book incarnate in these four limbs, these two eyes and small voice. The boy did not know that Paulus might be his father. Will had not been so bold. Paulus wanted to tell him, and he burned on the forks of a problem. Duty spoke with the voice he had always heeded; the dawning reality of kinship, and the small hope he held of being able to face his maker, spoke in quietly unanswerable opposition.

Paulus remembered sunrises slanting in through the cobwebby windows of Andrew's tack shed. Had Andrew ever seen Paulus on the streets of The Fells, thought to hail him perhaps? Had he told Andrew of his plan to buy the forgetting?

The sun was not yet up. Will was moving around just outside the door, and Paulus could hear the deep, even breaths of the boy. His boy. The sixth of Myros' collection.

Paulus stretched. He had not slept under a roof in more than a month, and his body was aging past the point when it could easily absorb a month on the campaign. The scars along his ribs hurt, and his shoulders popped, and in an instant of quiet revelation he understood that Myros had collected children, and Paulus had killed them, because Myros wanted the dragon Paulus had killed four years before.

Will had a copy of the Book on a tree-stump table beside his hearth. It was still too dark to read, but Paulus paged through the Book anyway, soothing himself with the beads in his fingers and the familiar weight and texture of the faith he had known all his life. He thought he was looking for something in the Book, but he did not know what, and when enough light had returned to the sky that he could discern the words, he set the Book aside and went to his saddlebag for whetstone and oil.

Sharpening his sword, Paulus imagined the boy grown into a soldier, and was filled with a black fury at what the world had done to him. No, he thought. The boy slept as only a child can, still as death, unstirred by the scrape of the whetstone. Memories rode in on the tide of Paulus' anger. In the Book was a story of a girl named Lily, saved by a story whispered in her ear while she was sleeping. Thinking of it, Paulus found his own tongue loosening. A story came to him, and as he remembered it he told it to the boy.

IX: The Jester's Story

Legend had it that the commoners' gift of magic came from the gods' anger at the separation of people into high and low. Like all legends, this one was as good an explanation as any, and the kingdom largely subscribed to it. One bit of magic, to be deployed once and only once, whether foolish or wise: this was the commoner's reward for a lifetime of subservience. The jester found this delicious, and wasted no opportunity to crow over the kingdom's fatuous belief. But the jester had secrets, and reasons.

Much of his life was apparent in the topology of his face. The king's common subjects bore an expression of calm security, a faith in their sovereign and in their one bit of magic to see them through whatever demands life would place upon them. But as if he had been built by one of the angry gods, the jester's face quirked and twisted with freshly remembered regret, and his cast eye, forever looking vacantly away to his right, took on a horrible aspect when his humor turned scabrous and biting. The younger princes and princesses fled the throne room at his every entrance, pushing each other in most ignoble haste, and the queen reluctantly took action when the youngest prince, awakening in mortal fear from a nightmare of the jester's crooked eye and whiplash tongue, ran blindly from his room and broke both of his legs in a fall down a flight of stairs.

Only a few hours later, in the throne room, the queen looked sadly from her liege lord to his *memento mori*, telling each that the safety of the royal progeny outweighed decades of service and reward. "His loyalty to you speaks well of him," she said to the king. "Even your dog is not so loyal."

The old dog looked up at her, the tip of his tail twitching. The jester thought that if he had had a tail, it might have twitched as well.

The queen spoke more than she knew, and behind his beard the king mused. The jester farted outrageously and refused to say a word, but within the scrawny rack of his chest, his heart beat with both fear and love for the queen who at that moment was proposing that he be pensioned off to a mountain barony safely away from tender gazes. His love for her exceeded the bounds even of his love for ruler and kingdom, and in that moment the jester bitterly regretted the day when he had loosed his one bit of magic to save the king.

Outside the castle walls, the jester sat crosslegged against a dead tree, looking out over the shore of a lake whose surface was rippled like an old window. He was tired of conjuring witty deflating comments. Tired of handstands, tired of juggling the skulls of the king's would-be assassins. He'd grown old, found aches in his joints and sleepless nights at the end of every day. There were many things he wished had never happened.

The jester had not always been a jester, any more than the king had been a king or the king's dog had been a dog. The day the old king died, the crown prince sat a silent vigil by his father's body until midnight, when he leapt to his feet and went to the chamber door. "Tomorrow a barred door closes on me," he said to his guard. "Tonight I walk through my city."

In the marketplace the uncrowned king walked among his subjects. He flirted with shop girls, bought perhaps one too many flagons of wine, and found himself in the shadow of the city walls watching a pair of ragged street performers. They were tired and performed reluctantly, but he gave them the strength of gold thrown at their feet. When the first birds had begun to chirp in anticipation of the dawn, the pair of acrobats were still turning their tumbles and mining their repertoire for tricks this munificent stranger had not yet seen.

Few things travel faster then news of a king's death, and the two weary acrobats were attuned to town gossip as only itinerant clowns can be. The older brother had absorbed the news and let it find a resting place in his mind; the younger had grown consumed with desire to avenge an injustice perpetrated by the dead king many years before, when an unlucky circus ringmaster had made an inopportune comment about the old king's cleft palate. One thing that travels faster than news of royal death is tidings of royal insult, and before long the ringmaster had vanished into the castle dungeon as his two boys performed with masklike faces before their sovereign, who rose at the end to pronounce the show the most excellent he'd seen in many a year.

The older son had made his peace with this. One lived in one's world, and one did not insult the king. The younger, though, turned the injustice inward and fed on it, not realizing that it was also feeding on him. Over a span of ten years man and hatred grew more to look like one another, and at last on a breezy summer night with dew on the ivy that climbed the city walls, the younger brother, addled with fantasies of regicide, saw his chance for revenge.

It would be their final routine, the brothers told their sole watcher. Dawn was coming, and besides they knew no trick to better it.

The uncrowned king accepted this. "I have been well entertained," he said, "and who better than you to know when you have no more to give?"

Nodding, the brothers unfolded a leather package containing ten knives. "Ready?" the older asked.

"We should rehearse it once."

"Start with three, then."

The king couldn't be certain whether the clowns were really so uncertain of this routine, or whether the uncertainty was part of their patter. Predawn gleam flashed on the knife blades as they flickered between the two brothers in a pattern almost intelligible. "Marvelous," the king said. "I imagine that's dangerous given your eye. Can you see out of it?"

Only for a moment, an eyeblink or even less, a long-dormant sense of hurt bloomed in the older brother. His life had given him a keen sense of irony, and it never escaped his notice when audiences tossed comments toward him of the sort that had gotten his father killed. The pain passed almost immediately, but not before causing a tremor in his throwing hand.

Blades clashed as the younger brother knocked the errant throw from the air. "Careful, brother," he said. The older brother blinked.

"Well enough," he lied. "I see well enough."

Six knives again, this time flawless for thirty seconds. Then the younger brother said, "Now four. Now." Together they stooped, and the gleaming pattern between them recomplicated itself just long enough for the king to think *Masterful.* Then the younger brother cried out and dropped his knives in a clatter. One of them bounded toward the king, who reached to pick it up.

"Not to worry, Your Majesty," the younger brother said. He stooped to retrieve the knife, and just as it registered in the king's mind that this slim and smiling trickster knew who he was — had watched him from crowds since he was old enough to assume the paste crown of First Successor — the younger brother leaned in low and thrust the knife into the king's belly.

What should have followed then was a lingering death and a hasty scampering escape over the city walls, but the uncrowned king was not quite the fool the younger acrobat had thought him. His mail shirt, forged within subterranean earshot of the cell where the old ringmaster had died wishing for sunlight, caught the blade and held it with only an inch of its tip parting skin and muscle. The younger brother's weight bore the king over, and he lay on his back, struggling to catch his breath and looking calmly into the eyes of his assassin.

"This blood," the younger brother said, holding his cut hand so the blood dripped onto the king's face. "It is my father's, and I will avenge it." He drew another knife from his belt.

"You are older than I am," the king said. "I do not know your father. Your grievance is with a dead man."

"When you are dead," the younger brother said, "I will have no grievance." He planted one knee in the king's chest. His brother called his name.

"Kill me, then," said the king. "But know that you redress no wrong. You kill as a mad dog kills, because you don't know what else to do."

Perhaps the younger brother hesitated for a moment, or perhaps magic saw its opportunity and spoke through his elder sibling's mouth; but before the knife could fall the older brother said, "You will not be a mad dog, brother. You will not repay shame with shame."

With those words, his life's one bit of magic whirlpooled from his body, and where a moment before the king had lain helpless under an assassin's knife, now the older brother watched as a small brown dog pawed at the king's tunic and strained to lick his chin.

The king pushed the dog aside and with a disgusted noise jerked the knife from the broken links of his mail. "Did you know who I was?" he asked.

The remaining brother, three knives in his two dangling hands, shook his head.

"It is odd," the king said, and had to pause for breath. He struggled to his feet. "To thank a man who would turn his brother into a dog."

"Odder yet to save the son of the man who killed my father," the older brother replied.

The king looked from the older brother to the attentive dog, who limped ever so slightly on one front paw. "So," he said.

"But I have seen men die, and few were able to face it as you did," the older brother went on. He began to gather up his props and gimmicks. "I thought I saw a kingly man in you." He tried to say something more, but he could not speak of what he had done.

The dog sat in front of the king. His tail wagged against one of the fallen knives, and he started up at the clatter and ran a few steps before returning with tail and nose both low to the ground. "Take care of my brother," said the lone acrobat as he shouldered his pack. "I see he wishes to remain with you."

"Why should I not kill him?"

The acrobat looked the king in the eye. "Your grievance is not with a dog."

Dawn broke on the castle's highest towers.

"True," said the king. "Very well, he will remain with me. As will you. I will have you and your brother at my throne, one to remind me of how close to death I came, and the other to remind me of why I was allowed to live. Walk with me, king's jester."

All of this was bad enough; but then the jester fell in love with the queen.

He remembered the moment of falling in love like a story told by someone else. The great stones of the hall outside the throne room, pale gray except streaks on either side, where generations of the royal wolfhounds had rubbed their ears along the grooves and ridges in the ancient stones. This king, whose life the jester had saved, was the first in memory to keep a limping brown dog of anonymous pedigree instead of the great loping hounds named for stars and mythical ancestors.

Passing her in the hall: she taller by a head and younger by two generations, he favoring a heel bruised earlier that day tumbling for an ambassador. She with hair the color of the old streaks in the walls, a brown almost black, and eyes the color of the untouched stones, the gray of a cloud heavy with lightning; he with a balding head and knuckles swollen by winter's chill. The jester became exalted in that moment, realizing that she was the castle, she was the kingdom, it was the twin example of her kindness and her iron rectitude that made it possible for the king to spare the jester's brother. He loved her because she seemed in that moment to him like an ideal given flesh, an ideal for which the sacrifice of a brother was not too great. Foolish, yes, and sentimental: but as good an explanation as any.

It haunted the jester that he had been willing to kill his brother. And he had; only the fickleness of magic had sped his mouth and stayed his hand. He found some small comfort in the royal heir's person, his utter lack of resemblance to his father. The old king had been capricious, vindictive, wanton in both kindness and cruelty. His successor remained scrupulous and fair, even generous. Around him the kingdom prospered without war.

And I didn't kill my brother, the jester thought. I saved him. I protected him, as an older brother must.

The king's dog was old now, gray around the muzzle and lame in his hind legs. A superstition arose that the king would live only as long as his dog (no one said this about the jester), and although the king knew better, still he protected the dog's life as jealously as his own, lest its death provoke unrest in the kingdom. The irony of this kept the jester in fine form for the mordant humor expected of him at court.

What would happen, he wondered, if the king were actually persuaded to foist him off on some rustic baron? Sooner or later, wouldn't the story of the dog his brother leak between the royal lips? And wouldn't the queen . . . ? The duty of her heart was to her husband, and of her mind to her king. She would have the dog killed out of a kind of loathing mercy, pitying the beast its lost humanity even as she ordered it drowned to ensure that no entombed memory would resurface and tear out the throat of the sleeping king.

Having once thought this, the jester grew certain events could play out no other way, just as having once seen the queen as his own ideals bodied forth he could never rid himself of his passion for her. Exaltation fled him. "Why must I love her?" he demanded of the sky, but the clouds of course took on the color of her eyes and kept their peace. Love twisted inside him the way magic had on its way from his body, anguish and ecstasy. Loving the queen who would kill his brother, the jester could only think of her implacable magnificence, her mind like light in cold water.

It was afternoon. The jester left the lake, went back to the city and the castle, and the next day the queen mentioned it again. Wouldn't the old jester be happier away from the trials and pressures of court? She asked, slipping through the fissure in his field of vision, and the jester knew what he had to do.

The spell broker kept himself secret, but the jester knew where to find him in the twilit side of the city. "My magic is gone," the jester said.

"Else why would you be here?" the broker said, and displayed brown teeth in a round white face shaved smooth as an egg. "Let me look at you."

The jester kept himself still as the spell broker plucked a strand of his hair and burned it over a candle, traced the outline of his ribs, smelled his breath, looked into his eyes and ears. "What is it you want?" the broker said upon finishing his inspection.

"The safety of my brother." The jester had heard stories about the deviousness of the spell broker. It was best not to be too specific too soon.

"Safety. Magic cannot guarantee safety. Magic can sometimes kill a threat, perhaps redirect it. Forgetting-magic is the easiest, though, and the surest."

She could forget, the jester thought. It made him inexplicably sad, though, the idea of court whispers: the queen, forget? She of the searchlight mind and unshakable will, the grey eyes like stones that held within them memories of each and every soul who passed by?

I will protect my brother.

"Forgetting magic, yes," the jester said. "If it is the easiest, it must come cheaply."

"The cheapest magic comes dear," said the broker.

"Name your price."

"Your eye."

"Very well," the jester said, and in a sudden panic thought *too soon, spoke too soon*, because the broker was still speaking, and the words out of his mouth were, "Your left eye."

My good eye, the jester thought. How will I look on the queen?

But his mouth was already open saying yes.

He found he could look upon the queen, after a fashion. If he positioned himself correctly, she would, on her way to kiss the king, walk through the part of his world that had not faded to a lifeless fog. He could not see her clearly, only well enough to remember how she had once appeared to him.

Well enough.

I did this for you, he would whisper sometimes under his breath. *So you would not feel betrayed when you discovered what I have done for my brother.*

In the jester's thirty-seventh year, when the dog his brother was thirty-three, the king had retired him from acrobatics, and the jester passed his days in excremental assaults on courtiers even as he kept his head turned slightly away to the left of the queen. The court thought him blind in the right eye instead of the left, and grudgingly credited him for his seemly deference to the queen's presence. They imagined that this deference arose out of gratitude at being permitted to remain at court, and the queen's stature increased among the aristocratic gossips, her reputation for kindness burnishing the well-known brilliance of her mind and the much-praised symmetry of her face. She often stooped to pet the old dog, who would thump his tail against the leg of the throne at her approach.

The jester kept his secrets, and he was careful around the children. The broker's spell made no guarantee against the queen's remembering. If he pitied himself from time to time, he ran his fingers where the queen's had been, along the dog his brother's neck, and he said to himself, unable to stop: *One lives in one's world*, he said to the sleeping dog. *One lives in one's world.*

X: The Boy

The boy still slept. But Will had come in from outside. "You're not blind," he said.

"I'm not a dog, either," Paulus said. He set Will's copy of the Book aside.

Will lit his pipe. "Twice someone spent their magic on you?"

"Aye," Paulus said. "Twice."

"And how did the second come about?"

"You wouldn't believe me," Paulus said.

"Already I don't believe you," Will said. "Tell another one."

"My brother confessed to the queen and as a reward for the laughter he had brought to the court, she bought me back my shape as a man, on the condition that I enter the king's service. I fought eleven years in the king's wars, and then he sent me to kill the dragon. When I came back, my brother and the king had both died, and I was released. Since then I have been for hire."

Will blew smoke rings over the sleeping boy. "All of this after you tried to kill the king? Ha," he said. "I wish that was true. No, I don't."

Three times, actually, Paulus thought. The forgetting he'd bought four years ago in The Fells was the third. Paulus made an occasional pastime of imagining who that little bit of magic had come from: a gambler needing to cover a debt, a soldier wanting a woman, a merchant whose cargo had foundered in the straits. Perhaps even the woman who had borne this child who might be his. The brokers of The Fells moved through the hamlets and farms of the mountains, following the lucrative scents of poverty and desperation. Their prices weren't fair, but even a rapacious deal often made the difference between feeding children and selling them.

"Three years ago?" he asked.

"Four, in the fall."

"How?"

Will shrugged. "She was bringing water. Sat down for a rest beside the path, I guess, and I found her when I heard the boy crying. Maybe six months old, he was."

Could be, Paulus thought. The sleeping boy was curled on his side, arms drawn in under his chin, still shadowed from the sunlight falling through the hut's single window. Firelight glowed in the tangles of his hair. Paulus thought he might see something of himself in the shape of the boy's shoulders, the line of his jaw.

Today I must kill Myros, he thought. Because if I do not, I will have to kill this boy, and I cannot.

"Have you named him? Had she?"

"She called him after you," Will said. "So I did, too."

Paulus was brimful and shattering. A boy with my name, he thought. After all this, all the leavings and the years with no place to call my own, in my fiftieth year I ride out on a mission of killing and find a boy with my name.

It was written in the Book: *Let the Lesson be.*

He stood, and his knees cracked. "Today this ends," Paulus said. "One way or another. If the boy asks for me, tell him I will return by nightfall or not at all."

The boy. Still, Paulus admonished himself, you cannot call him by his name?

He walked the final steps of his Agate Tower errand, his body leading him to the dragon's cave as if his scars were lines on a map. It would have taken Myros some time to prepare the spell to control the dragon, and more time yet for him to gather his courage and enter the cave when the dragon did not come out. Quite a string of surprises Myros was in for, Paulus thought, and bared his teeth as he wound up a switchbacking footpath that ended on the ridge above the cave. He made no effort to disguise his presence. If Myros had already spent his energy on the spell, then he was just another baby turtle; if he had not, Paulus was in for a hard fight, but on this day he would kill no man from behind. He crested the ridge and closed his eyes, riding out a wave of memories. The cave mouth, like a half-lidded eye, was the same, yet it seemed smaller to him; the smell of the snow on the north side of the ridge made him think of ice storms rattling against a window with a sound like the rasp of the dragon's scales.

They were all before him now, the specters of those gone from his life: his brother, Andrew, his mother, the king. Men he had served with. Joy. And the boy she had named for him.

When Paulus opened his eyes, Myros was looking at him from the cave entrance. "For this you made me kill children," Paulus said.

"I made you do nothing," Myros said, and made a gesture with his ringed hand.

Paulus was alight with pain: every blade that had ever cut him cut him anew. He felt the teeth of dogs and the dragon's talons, the piercing of an arrow and the grate of a spearpoint across his skull. Thumbs gouged at his eyes, and bootheels ground his fingers. He dropped his sword and felt his knees buckle. Blood roared in his ears, and somewhere beyond it he heard Myros' footsteps on the stones of the trail. Looking up through tears, he saw the apprentice coming nearer. You misjudge me, Paulus thought, and drank of his pain until it had given him strength to stand, and when he had gotten to his feet he left his sword where it lay and fell upon Myros with bare hands.

When it was done, he lay gasping on the stony ground as the apprentice's spell slowly faded from his body. He felt as if he was being knit together again, and when the pain had faded into the leaden dullness that for Paulus always followed killing, he got to his feet. Leaving his sword where it lay, he walked a short distance into the cave, to the point where the light from without finally failed. Trailing away into the dark, the bones of the dragon had already begun taking on the color of the stones around them.

One more, Paulus remembered thinking. I was right, and I was wrong.

It was afternoon when he returned to Will's farm. The boy was on his hands and knees following an insect through the beaten grass. He looked up at Paulus' approach and stood. "There's a beetle there," he said.

Paulus knew in that moment how little he understood of children, and how enormous his task was. "Your name is Paulus. Is that right?" he asked.

The boy nodded, but his attention was already wandering back to the beetle. He parted the grasses looking for it.

"My name is Paulus too."

The boy looked over his shoulder at Paulus. Where, Paulus wondered? A place without wizards. A place without these bargains driven for your soul. A place where my boy will not follow my path. He realized he had forgotten his sword, and resolved that he would never wear another. Let the Lesson be.

"You're going to come with me," Paulus said.

And the boy said, "Where are we going?"